"DO YOU WANT TO PERISH?"

Sarah read aloud from right to left, translating from Hebrew to English as she went: "'The Seers will be torn. There will be those among them who deny the Chosen One to her face . . . yet those Seers will surely perish.'" She looked up at the boy. "Is that what you want? Do you want to perish?"

The boy didn't reply. Instead he began to twitch.

His hands flew to his throat. His face turned bright red—and all at once enormous black splotches appeared on his arms. Blood dripped from his nose, from his ears. . . . He opened his mouth in a silent scream, but his lips turned to liquid.

He collapsed into a heap of black slime.

Sarah's jaw dropped. A rush of guilt and horror swept over her. *He didn't even have time to deny me again.* She knew the prophecy would come true—but she had no idea it would be so instantaneous, so dramatic . . . so terrifying. She didn't want to prove herself like this; she didn't want anyone to actually *die*. But she thrust the regrets aside. She had to seize the moment. The boy's sudden vaporization did accomplish something: It confirmed the truth.

"Take a good look," she breathed. She cast a long glance at the crowd, now silent and terrified. "All of you can see for yourself. I *am* the Chosen One."

About the Author

Daniel Parker is the author of over twenty books for children and young adults. He lives in New York City with his wife, a dog, and a psychotic cat named Bootsie. He is a Leo. When he isn't writing, he is tirelessly traveling the world on a doomed mission to achieve rock-and-roll stardom. As of this date, his musical credits include the composition of bluegrass sound-track numbers for the film *The Grave* (starring a bloated Anthony Michael Hall) and a brief stint performing live rap music to baffled Filipino audiences in Hong Kong. Mr. Parker once worked in a cheese shop. He was fired.

COUNT DOWN

MAY

by
Daniel Parker

Simon & Schuster
www.SimonSays.com/countdown/

First Aladdin Paperbacks edition April 1999

 Produced by 17th Street Productions,
a division of Daniel Weiss Associates, Inc.
33 West 17th Street, New York, NY 10011

Cover design by Mike Rivilis

Aladdin Paperbacks
An imprint of Simon & Schuster
Children's Publishing Division
1230 Avenue of the Americas
New York, NY 10020

Library on Congress Cataloging-in-Publication Data
Parker, Daniel, 1970–
May / by Daniel Parker. — 1st Aladdin Paperbacks ed.
p.   cm. — (Countdown ; 5)
Summary: The Visionaries are plagued by locusts and the cruise ship *Majestic*
voyages toward the United States bearing the Chosen One.
ISBN 0-689-81823-8 (pbk.)
[1. Supernatural—Fiction.] I. Title. II. Series: Parker, Daniel, 1970–
Countdown ; 5.
PZ7.P2243May   1999
[Fic]—dc21   99-14012
CIP   AC

To Jim and Alex

The Ancient Scroll of the Scribes:

In the fifth lunar cycle,
During the months of Iyar
and Sivan in the year 5759,
The servants of the Demon will
produce miracles after miracles,
Attributing signs and wonders
to the False Prophet.
And all the while the Chosen One
will draw closer to the Demon.
The Demon's powers will grow on earth,
And she will revel in her new human form.
The Seers will be torn.
There will be those among them who
deny the Chosen One to her face,
Yet those Seers will surely perish.
The Chosen One and her followers
will have a traitor in their midst,
And the Chosen One will lead her
companions to death and ruin.
Again the Chosen One will suffer,
And again she will be saved.

Lift our seats unless we trip, so drink in our volcano.
Adultery stirs him. We demand a
marker for strikes. Cremate us.
Five two ninety-nine.

The countdown has started . . .

The long sleep is over.

For three thousand years I have patiently watched and waited. The Prophecies foretold the day when the sun would reach out and touch the earth—when my slumber would end, when my ancient weapon would breathe, when my dormant glory would blaze once more upon the planet and its people.

That day has arrived.

But there can be no triumph without a battle. Every civilization tells the same story. Good requires evil; redemption requires sin. The legends are as varied as are the civilizations that spawned them— yet each contains that same nugget of truth.

So I am not alone. The Chosen One awaits me. The flare opened the inner eyes of the Visionaries, those who can join the Chosen One to prevent my reign. But in order for them to defeat me, they must first make sense of their visions.

For you see, every vision is a piece of a puzzle, a puzzle that will eventually form a picture . . . a picture that I will shatter into a billion pieces and reshape in the image of my choosing.

I am prepared. My servants knew of this day. They made the necessary preparations to confuse the Visionaries—all in anticipation of that glorious time when the countdown ends and my ancient weapon ushers in the New Era.

My servants unleashed the plague that reduced the earth's population to a scattered horde of frightened adolescents. None of these children know how or why their elders and youngers perished.

And that was only the beginning.

My servants have descended upon the chaos. They will subvert the Prophecies in order to convert the masses into unknowing slaves. They will hunt down the Visionaries, one by one, until all are dead. They will eliminate the descendants of the Scribes so that none of the Visionaries will learn of the scroll. The hidden codes shall remain hidden. Terrible calamities and natural disasters will wreak havoc upon the earth. Even the Chosen One will be helpless against me.

I *will* triumph.

PART I:

May 1-10, 1999

CHAPTER
ONE

The room hummed with an incessant, electric drone.

Outside, the sun might have been shining and a crisp morning wind might have been blowing—but in here, in this cavernous place, the climate remained perfectly static. The flickering blue twilight never faded. And it never would because the muted television sets that lined the walls in precise four-by-four grids would never be extinguished.

Somebody was always watching them. Always.

At this particular moment Trevor Collins found that very reassuring.

He sat alone on a chair in a corner, focused on the pale girl whose face filled one of the screens. She was screaming—her full ruby lips flapping in silent fury, her jet black curls twisted in matted disarray. Yet he couldn't bring himself to turn up the volume. He couldn't bring himself to hear her words.

He was frightened.

The fear was irrational; he knew that. She certainly couldn't *do* anything. Not only was she locked in the special high-security cell, but he'd also locked *this* door—the sole entrance to his special inner sanctum,

4

the command center from which he monitored his perfect little community. She couldn't escape, of course. Unless she suddenly acquired superhuman strength, there was no way she could break through an electronically sealed, two-inch-thick steel door.

Was there?

Trevor swallowed. He ran a hand through his greasy, unkempt brownish blond hair. He hadn't showered or changed in days. To stew in his own filth was not at all like him. Control and self-discipline were the cornerstones of his success. Without them he never would have survived after the plague that killed every adult on the planet, let alone built a new utopian society. But now . . . he'd hardly left this room since it happened. Since his girlfriend freaked out almost a week ago. He couldn't tear his eyes off . . . *her*—this stranger with the face he knew so well. And the more he watched, the more certain he became that the old Jezebel Howe was gone forever.

Then again, he didn't really know who the old Jezebel *was,* did he?

She wore a hundred different faces. She was such an *actress*—a manipulative fake who did whatever was necessary to get what she wanted. But she was beautiful. And she was *his.* Or at least she pretended to be his. Still, that was good enough.

What happened to you?

Even after five straight days of observation, he was no closer to figuring out the nature of her psychosis. It was so sinister, so *ugly.* He leaned forward and peered at the screen. At least she seemed to be calming down a little. The movement of her lips was

5

settling into a pattern . . . as if she were repeating the same word over and over again.

Trevor?

Yes. She was calling his name.

With a trembling finger he reached out and pushed the volume button.

". . . Trevor!" she yelled. Her voice sounded flat and tinny in the speaker. "Trevor, you better start listening. Turn up those TVs."

He winced. Why did it suddenly seem as if she could read his mind, as if she always knew what he was doing? ESP was impossible. He didn't believe in *any* kind of supernatural nonsense; that garbage was for his sister, Ariel, and her spaced-out, druggie friends. He believed in *science*—the kind of science he'd used to build this campus up from nothing.

"Listen to me," she snarled. "If you don't let me out of this cell, there's gonna be hell to pay. Mark my words."

Trevor's eyes involuntarily flashed to the rifle lying at his feet. He could never hurt her; he knew that. But if she somehow managed to escape . . .

She can't escape! She can't see you or hear you! Relax!

And then she smiled.

"You aren't going to let me go, are you?" she asked. Her tone was quite calm—almost friendly. "You think I'm some kind of lunatic. You still think I'm Jezebel, don't you?"

Trevor held his breath.

"I see." She sighed. "Well, then, it looks like you're going to have to suffer the consequences. I'm sorry it has to happen this way. But there's nothing I can do to stop it at this point. There's really no other solu—"

The screen went dead.

What the hell? Trevor bolted out of his chair. His eyes darted around the room.

Half the screens were blank.

He leaned forward and savagely jabbed the power button. No response. His breath started coming fast. This was all wrong; he'd just checked the wiring last week. He tried another TV. Nothing happened. The rest of the laboratory complex was now cut off from him. All sorts of kids were locked in here—sick kids, criminals, crazy kids who believed in the Chosen One . . . kids whom he couldn't see now. Including Jezebel. If there was a power failure, then they could do anything they wanted. Anything.

An urgent pounding rattled the door.

"Trevor?" a shaky voice cried.

"Who is it?" he barked. He reached for his rifle.

"Barney," came the frightened reply. "You better come out here. There's . . . I don't know. Something bad."

"What?" Trevor demanded. The cold metal of the barrel and trigger felt good against his moist fingers. He couldn't panic; he was too strong. He was a leader. He needed to calm himself, to focus. "What's going on?"

"You better see for yourself."

Gripping the rifle tightly, Trevor dashed across the room and burst into the hall.

The lights were out. The lack of fluorescence left

the hall eerily silent. Bright early morning sunshine sliced across the linoleum from the small windows in the classroom doors—but the electricity had clearly been cut.

That meant Jezebel's door was unlocked.

"The-they're outside," Barney stammered.

"They?" Trevor glanced at him. Barney's jowly face was even more pale than usual. His beady blue eyes were wide. He clutched his own rifle so hard that Trevor could see the whites of his knuckles. "Who?"

Barney gulped. "Not who." He paused. *"What."*

"What do you mean, *what?"* Trevor scowled at him. "Give me a straight answer—"

"Come on," Barney interrupted. He jerked his head toward a stairwell at the end of the hall. "You can see from the second floor."

Before Trevor could say another word, Barney sprinted away from him.

Trevor's face darkened. *That imbecile!* He dashed down the hall, close on Barney's heels—and rage began to surpass his fear. His friends had no idea how to handle a crisis. They were all turning into fat, complacent slobs. The weapons and surveillance system had made them lazy and incompetent.

"It was so fast," Barney gasped. "They came all at once."

Trevor frowned as they clattered up the shadowy stairs. There was a strange noise in the air—almost like the hissing roar of a packed stadium . . . only with more of an annoying nasal quality. It didn't even sound human.

8

What *was* that?

Jezebel's words echoed through his mind: ". . . *you're going to have to suffer the consequences. . . . There's nothing I can do to stop it at this point.*"

Trevor shook his head. *No!* She could not be responsible for a power failure. It wasn't physically possible. She was locked in her cell when it happened.

The moment they reached the second-floor landing, Barney spun around and dashed toward a closed window at the end of the hall. The noise grew louder. Trevor followed, but he found his knees were shaking. The strange roar reached a fever pitch. Something was moving out there . . . it looked like a hailstorm, but one that fell in all directions: down *and* up. Cold terror washed over him.

"Look," Barney whispered. "Just look at them all."

Clenching his jaw, Trevor forced himself to march straight up to the glass.

"Holy *crap!*" he cried.

The entire campus was overrun with . . . bugs.

Huge, brown, flapping insects, a whole *cloud* of them. They swarmed over every surface, buzzing and squirming, bouncing against the windowpane. For a moment Trevor thought he might retch. The lawn outside the building was completely smothered. Not a spot of green was visible. His gaze frantically roved over to the barbed wire fence, to the power cables—just in time to catch a shower of sparks leaping into the air, followed by a sizzle and a cloud of smoke.

Hundreds of blackened creatures fell to the earth. They looked like oversized drops of polluted rain.

"They're chewing through the wiring," Barney murmured in a quivering voice. "They're ruining everything!"

Trevor shook his head. "What are they?" he breathed. "They look like—like grasshoppers. Is that what they are?"

"No. Not . . . really."

"Not *really?*"

Barney chewed his lip. His eyes darted to Trevor, then back to the grotesque, slithering brown sea before them.

"They're locusts."

TWO

Afternoon of May 3
Cruise Ship *The Majestic*,
South of Crete

Every bone in Sarah Levy's body ached with exhaustion. She'd slept only five hours in as many days. She literally felt as if the powerful ocean breeze could lift her off her feet and toss her over the back of the fast-moving ship. Her glasses were soiled; her insides heaved with every rise and plunge of the sun-washed deck. Yet she refused to show any weakness. Her features remained grimly set.

"Do you want to try to burn my scroll one more time?" she cried over the wind and the rumble of the massive turbines. "Do you?"

Forty-five armed and uniformed teenage soldiers stared back at her, their faces blank.

She knew that the confrontation was inevitable. Only a few among them believed the wild rumors about her ancient parchment and the prophecies within . . . and so the time had come to prove herself once again—in front of as many witnesses as possible.

She was certain she would.

There was nothing to fear anymore. She held the

yellowed scroll in both hands, cradling it as if it were a royal scepter. And in a way, it was. It was the symbol of the authority she alone possessed, the key to hidden knowledge that could save them all. Even though every single one of these boys carried a machine gun, she carried something far more powerful—something whose nature she was only beginning to comprehend.

"Do you want to imprison me again?" she yelled.

Nobody answered. Only a few among them could speak English. But the *meaning* of her words should have been obvious. Her harsh inflection communicated the message. She was not to be abused any longer. She was not to be thrown into a cell with a hundred other starving kids. She was to be treated with the utmost care and respect . . . if any of them wanted a true chance at survival.

"*Qu'est-ce que tu veux?*" one of them suddenly called.

Sarah frowned.

"He wants to know what you want," another translated.

Sarah shifted the scroll in her hands, seizing it by the worn wooden handles. Drawing on the last of her strength, she raised it above her head and unfurled a small portion of the parchment, revealing the delicately drawn Hebrew characters.

"Tell him that I want you all to accept the truth and power of these prophecies," she stated. "I want you to throw your guns overboard and free all the kids you locked away—"

A deafening burst of explosions cut her off.

The pegs jerked violently. She flinched, losing her grip. The scroll fell behind her. She spun—and her eyes widened in horror.

The parchment was riddled with bullet holes.

"Allons-y!" several people cried. *"Allons-y!"*

There was a clatter of boots. The deck vibrated under Sarah's feet. In an instant she was surrounded, a dozen machine guns thrust in her face. But she could only gape at the ruined scroll, the miraculous artifact that had been damaged beyond repair. . . .

"It can't be," she whispered in desperation. "It can't be—"

One of the bullet holes closed.

Sarah's eyes narrowed.

Was her mind playing tricks on her?

A gasp rose from the soldiers.

"Regardez!" one hissed.

No, no . . . as if answering her unspoken prayers, the frayed puncture marks began to disappear, vanishing in rapid succession. *My God!* The terror pumping through her veins turned to a wild joy. It almost appeared as if the parchment were made of living tissue—a tissue that could heal itself faster than that of any creature on earth.

"See?" she cried. "See? What did I tell you? You can't destroy it!"

The guns began to drop away.

Within seconds the scroll had been restored to its original state. Even the old *stains* reappeared. The text was intact. Yes! Sarah tore her eyes from the parchment, sweeping the shocked faces of the soldiers with her gaze. Any trace of their professionalism was gone. Now they were showing themselves for what they truly were: a pack of frightened teenagers.

"*C'est n'est pas possible,*" one of them whimpered. "*C'est pas—*"

"Shut up!" another interrupted.

Sarah sneered. It was the British soldier who had first imprisoned her, the one who had tried to burn the scroll several days ago. His pale face was etched with fear and disbelief. And Sarah couldn't help but feel pleased. He *deserved* to be scared—after everything he'd done to her, after everything he and the rest of the soldiers had done to the poor kids on this ship.

"Who are you?" he whispered.

She took a deep breath. "I'm . . ."

But the response hung in the air, unfinished. She held her breath. She couldn't quite bring herself to actually *say* the words—because the answer carried such a terrible weight.

I'm the Chosen One.

She still had no idea what the title truly meant. She had no idea what her ultimate role was to be. She only knew that she had a responsibility she couldn't begin to fathom . . . a responsibility for every last person left on earth. She only knew that she couldn't afford to be weak or selfish anymore. The prophecies concerning the survival of the human race centered around *her.* The indestructible scroll proved it.

Finally she exhaled. "I guess we'll all find out soon enough."

The soldier swallowed. "Wha-what do you want from us?" he stammered.

"Like I said, I want you to throw your guns overboard," she stated. "I want you to release all the people who lost the lottery, because they're coming with us."

"But that can't happen," he interrupted shakily. "Please. You must understand. There simply aren't enough supplies for all of us—"

"Then we'll *get* some!" she shouted. "But don't think for a second that you have the right to decide who goes and who stays. The lottery is over. We're *all* going. You say that the melting plague hasn't hit America, that there's still a government there. You say that it's a paradise. If that's true, then everybody deserves a shot at survival." Her voice tightened. *"Everybody.* Understand?"

He hesitated for a moment, then nodded. The rest of the soldiers were staring at him. He glanced around the deck. *"Jetez les fusils à la mer!"* he shouted. *"Maintenant!"*

Nobody moved.

"Maintenant!" he snapped. With that, he pushed his way through the crowd and hurled his machine gun over the railing. It spun end over end for several seconds—a twirling black baton against the deep blue afternoon sky—and fell out of sight.

Sarah held her breath.

A moment later the rest of the soldiers began to

do the same, unleashing a shower of weapons that plunged into the frothy green-blue water.

Not one of them uttered a word of complaint.

Finally. She allowed herself a quiet sigh of relief. *We're all acting like human beings. No more intimidation. No more beatings. No more violence—*

There was a muffled sound under the deck.

Sarah strained her ears. It was the unmistakable thump of running feet. She turned and glanced at the closed stairwell door, not ten feet away from her. *Uh-oh.* People were coming up the steps. Had the soldiers tricked her? Were there more of them on board?

"Sarah?" a deep, frightened voice called. "Sarah, are you all right?"

"Ibrahim!" she shouted. Relief washed over her. "Ibrahim, up here!"

The door flew open.

Ibrahim sprinted onto the deck—bare chested, his muscular arms outstretched, his handsome dark face aglow with a wide smile. And for the first time in her life, Sarah was *happy* to see him. No, she was elated. Even when he had rescued her from the bowels of this ship, she'd been far too confused and overwhelmed to feel much of anything. But now, as he threw his arms around her, she realized something.

Ibrahim Al-Saif is my best friend.

It was true. This strange Egyptian boy—this once devout Muslim who'd captured her and ultimately saved her, the boy whom she'd wanted to kill on many occasions . . . he was closer to her than anybody else at this moment. He'd kept her alive. He'd stood up to the soldiers. He'd believed in her from the very beginning. Not even her own family knew the truth about her—not her parents, not her dead brother, Josh. . . .

After a long embrace Ibrahim stepped back. "I heard shooting," he said breathlessly. "Are you all right?"

She nodded. "Where have you been?"

He waved his hand behind him. A mob of ragged-looking kids was filing out of the doorway. "Searching the ship for people like me," he answered.

"What do you mean?"

"Visionaries, Sarah." His smile widened. "I'm not alone. Other people have visions. Other people know of you, Sarah. People from all over the world, from different countries, who speak different languages." He turned to the kids, his voice rising. "Here she is!" he cried. "The Chosen One! *La fille choisie!*"

Sarah's mouth fell open. She couldn't believe it. *All* these kids knew of her? Her heart began to pound. She shot a quick glance at a few of them. Some appeared awed, others frightened, others troubled. . . . Finally her gaze came to rest on Aviva, the redheaded Israeli girl whom she and Ibrahim had met their first day on board. Aviva was the last one out the door—smiling and nodding, her hands clasped together as if she were praying. Tears filled her eyes.

"How?" Sarah breathed. "How did you find them?"

"Aviva was the first," Ibrahim whispered. "She told me she knew from her visions that the Chosen One was a girl. An *American* girl. But she never saw your face. Then we went through the ship. We asked *everybody*. It turns out—"

"That's not her," a voice interrupted.

Sarah's head jerked around. A tall blond boy stepped forward. He peered at her closely.

"What do you mean?" Ibrahim demanded.

The boy nervously licked his lips. His eyes darted over to the watchful soldiers. "Uh . . . I mean, I don't know what you're trying to pull." He pointed a shaky finger at Sarah. "But that girl isn't the Chosen One."

A few of the kids gasped.

Sarah grimaced. She found she was actually angry. Who was this guy to tell her she wasn't the Chosen One? After all, she had always been her own biggest skeptic. She was skeptical of *everything*. And *she* had been convinced of the truth. Had this kid read the scroll? Had he pored over the mountains of irrefutable evidence? Had he studied the prophecies? Had he seen the scroll burned and shot—only to be magically restored? Who did he think he was?

"How do you know?" she demanded.

"I've . . . seen this," he answered hesitantly. "I mean, I'm, like, having major déjà vu right now." He gestured around the deck. "See, I have this vision, where I, uh, see a phony Chosen One. And I, like, totally expose her in front of all these people. It's on a ship, too."

Sarah's face twisted in rage. *On a ship?* How convenient. Not only was this guy an inarticulate idiot, but people were actually listening to him. The awed looks were fading. Even the soldiers seemed a little less certain, a little more hesitant. She snatched the scroll off the ground.

"Let me read something to you," she snapped. She twisted the pegs counterclockwise until she reached the prophecies about the fifth lunar cycle. "Then let's see what you think."

Her eyes flashed down the passage. *Here we are. . . .*

She read aloud from right to left, translating from Hebrew to English as she went: "'The Seers will be torn. There will be those among them who deny the Chosen One to her face . . . yet those Seers will surely perish.'" She lifted her head. "Is that what you want? Do you want to perish?"

The boy didn't reply.

Instead he began to twitch.

His hands flew to his throat. His face turned bright red—and all at once enormous black splotches appeared on his arms. Blood dripped from his nose, from his ears. . . . He opened his mouth in a silent scream, but his lips turned to liquid.

Good Lord!

He collapsed into a heap of black slime.

Sarah's jaw dropped. A rush of guilt and horror swept over her. *He didn't even have time to deny me again.* She knew the prophecy would come true—but she had no idea it would be so instantaneous, so dramatic . . . so terrifying. She didn't want to prove herself like this; she didn't want anyone to actually *die*. But she thrust the regrets aside. She had to seize the moment. The boy's sudden vaporization did accomplish something: It confirmed the truth.

"Take a good look," she breathed. She cast a long glance at the crowd, now silent and terrified. "All of you can see for yourself. I *am* the Chosen One."

CHAPTER
THREE

**Babylon,
Washington
Morning of May 5**

What is up with all these goddamn bugs?

Ariel Collins stopped and swatted one of the grasshoppers out of her face. But as soon as it was gone, another one smacked against her cheek. She felt like screaming. The only problem was that she didn't want to open her mouth. If she did, one of the squirmy little things would fly right down her throat.

"How much farther?" Caleb Walker growled.

Ariel peeked over her shoulder. He stood right behind her, staring at the road—or what could be seen of it under the blanket of insects. Long, stringy brown hair shrouded his face. His pale forehead wrinkled in disgust. He was obviously pissed at her. And Ariel could definitely relate. She was pissed at everybody, too . . . not to mention tired and hungry and grossed out. It had taken *far* too long to get here.

"It's just up there, around the corner," she mumbled. She brushed a strand of brownish blond hair out of her eyes. She needed a haircut in a major way—she was starting to look more like a plant than a human being. "The driveway's on the next block."

Caleb didn't say anything. He glanced back down

21

the street—back toward the tired, sorry-looking bunch of losers bringing up the rear.

Ariel shook her head. *Man.* The sight of those kids was so damn depressing. She still couldn't believe that they were the only ones who had made it out of Seattle alive. There were twenty-two survivors in all, including Caleb and her . . . twenty-two lucky souls who managed to escape the inferno before burning to a crisp like hot dogs at a cookout.

"Sorry for yelling," Caleb finally muttered. "It's just . . . I don't know. I can't take much more of this."

I can't take much more of this, either.

What was she even *doing* in Babylon?

A week ago, when Seattle had suddenly gone up in flames for no apparent reason, coming back home seemed like a fine idea. Excellent, in fact. But now she felt like a grade-A moron. It was so *weird* to be back here, even without the bugs. And it wasn't the memories, either. She'd never been nostalgic—especially about this dump. No, it was more the fact that Babylon had turned into a ghost town. She hadn't seen a single kid. All she saw were the old, familiar split-level suburban homes and lame little strip malls . . . now looted, dark, and deserted.

And she couldn't help but ask herself: *Did Trevor shoot everybody? Did he just flip out and pump everyone full of lead?*

She shot a furtive look in the direction of the Washington Institute of Technology. The last time she was in the neighborhood, Trevor promised he would kill her on sight. What a guy. She wouldn't put it past her brother to become a serial killer or mass murderer.

No. Which was another reason they should probably just stop right now.

"What's going on?" a girl called from the back.

Ariel turned, frowning. *Oh, please.*

Leslie What's-her-face Tisch was running to catch up with them. Her stylish black boots crunched on the grasshoppers: *chomp, chomp, chomp.* It was amazing: Even after a week-long trek through the wilderness, Leslie looked as if she had stepped right out of a fashion shoot for some cheesy teen magazine. Well, except maybe for the bugs in her black curls. But her miniskirt was still in pretty good shape. Her olive skin was flawlessly clean, as always. Had that chick ever gotten one single zit in her entire life? Just *one?*

"Why did we stop?" Leslie asked. She glanced between Caleb and Ariel. "Is everything all right?"

"Sure," Ariel grumbled, turning her back and resuming her march toward the WIT campus. "If you don't mind getting grasshoppers up your nose." She knew that if she looked at Leslie for one more second, there was a very good chance she would smack her.

It would be so much fun to smack her, wouldn't it?

Hell, yes. Only she couldn't—because Leslie had saved her life.

Why her? Why didn't somebody else yank me out of that burning hotel?

It was so unfair!

Okay, okay. Ariel knew she couldn't drive herself crazy over it. She just had to be positive. Yeah. That was her new thing: positivity. Besides, the situation could have been worse, right? At least Leslie and

Caleb weren't fooling around anymore. Well, even if they *were*, Ariel wouldn't care that much. She didn't *like* Caleb. She just thought that Leslie had turned what had once been a very cute, very funny, very awesome guy into a blithering idiot.

But things were getting better. She was beginning to see flashes of the old Caleb every now and then. And in spite of the fact that Leslie was the most annoying person on the planet, she *was* being nice to Ariel. Everybody was. Of course, there was an obvious reason for that: None of these kids had ever been to Babylon, so they were all in Ariel's hands. Ariel had to admit something, too . . . it was pretty nice to be the one calling the shots again.

She was on top. Just like old times.

"Do you think there's gonna be bug spray or something at this place?" Leslie asked. "You know, like, insecticide?"

Ariel shrugged. How would *she* know?

She picked up her pace—mostly to get away from Leslie—but also because she could see a familiar metal plaque, half covered with grasshoppers, up ahead on the right side of the road:

THE WASHINGTON INSTITUTE OF TECHNOLOGY
BABYLON CAMPUS

We're here. I can't believe it.

Her stomach squeezed.

She slowed as she approached the open driveway gates. The last time she came to this place . . . *God.* It was a lifetime ago. She was still going out with

Brian. She was still friends with Jezebel. Jez was still going out with *Jack,* for God's sake—at least before Jack melted. So much had changed since that cold, rainy, miserable day in January. Everything, really. Brian had sworn he was going to come back and burn this place to the ground. For all she knew, Brian was dead now, too.

Caleb suddenly dashed ahead of her.

"Check it out!" he cried excitedly, waving his arm down the driveway. "The lights are on! People are there! Your brother must be home!"

Ariel stepped around the wrought iron doors and squinted through the cloud of insects. Caleb was right. Several windows glowed in the redbrick dormitory that stood at the end of the tree-lined drive. It was funny: The building looked just the way she remembered it—except for one crucial difference.

It was blocked off by a tall, shiny barbed wire fence.

Trevor. Yup. He was home, all right. Who else would have thought of such a heinous way to keep people out? Ariel stood on her toes and craned her neck. As far as she could see from here, the fence seemed to stretch across most of the lawn. It probably surrounded the entire campus.

"What's the matter?" Caleb asked. "What are we waiting for?"

She shot him a wary glance. "That fence is kind of making me nervous," she said.

Caleb frowned. "Why?"

"Yeah, Ariel," Leslie chimed in. "Why?"

Ariel rolled her eyes. "Because it wasn't there before. *That's* why."

"So?" Leslie smirked. "Maybe your brother wants to keep out the riffraff."

"Exactly," Ariel stated. She swatted another grasshopper out of her face. "That's what I'm trying to tell you."

Leslie sighed loudly. "Look, he's *your* brother. Just go in there and—"

"I told you about Trevor, all right?" Ariel interrupted. "He's a freak. And that's putting it nicely. He said he was gonna kill me."

"Then why the hell did you *bring* us here, Ariel?" Leslie barked. "You said that if you talked to him, you could work it out. Was that a lie?"

Ariel opened her mouth, then closed it. The rest of the kids were starting to catch up. They paused at the entrance—awkwardly avoiding Ariel's eyes. She glanced back at the dorm. *Was* it a lie? She wasn't sure. Back in Seattle, making peace with Trevor hadn't seemed quite so far-fetched. Then again, she'd been half out of her mind with booze and loneliness.

"Look, *somebody's* gotta go up there," Caleb said. "We're here. It's worth—"

He broke off in midsentence.

One of the dormitory doors had suddenly burst open.

Whoa.

A dark-haired kid bolted across the lawn toward the fence, spastically swatting bugs out of his eyes as he ran. He looked as if he were having a fit.

Ariel's eyes narrowed. "What—"

A loud, crisp *pop* echoed through the air.

"Get down!" Caleb shrieked.

26

Before Ariel could react, Caleb tackled her to the driveway. Dozens of grasshoppers squished under her body as she smacked against the pavement. *Eww!* She winced—not so much in pain, but because she thought she would yack. She could feel Caleb's hot breath against her ear. He was hyperventilating.

"What's going on?" she hissed. She couldn't see a damn thing. "Why—"

Another pop cut her off. It sounded like a cheap Fourth-of-July firecracker. A few people screamed. Bugs fluttered away. She could hear footsteps disappearing out the gates.

"Somebody's shooting at that kid," Caleb whispered.

Oh, God. Ariel swallowed. So Trevor really had gone crazy. But he wouldn't shoot at his own sister, would he? Would he? She squirmed out from under Caleb and stumbled to her feet—just in time to see the kid sprint past her.

"Get out!" the kid shouted. "Run for it!"

Ariel couldn't seem to move. She simply gaped at him—until Caleb seized her by the wrist and roughly yanked her back out onto the street. The next thing she knew, the three of them were running, close on the heels of Leslie and the others . . . and then they split off from the rest of the pack, turned a corner, and skidded to a halt.

"I don't know if this is safe," the boy gasped. He glanced fearfully behind him. "They might come after me."

"Is it Trevor?" Ariel choked out, struggling to catch her breath.

The boy snorted. "You kidding? Trevor wouldn't bother. He's too big for that. He'd get some other sicko to do it. . . ." His voice trailed off. He spun around, meeting Ariel's frightened gaze with a hard stare. "Hey, who the hell are *you?*" he demanded. "How do you know Trevor?"

Ariel took a step back. "I . . . well, I—"

"She's his sister," Caleb cut in, stepping between them. "What's going on?"

"His *sister?*" the boy spat. His face darkened.

"Wait, please," Ariel pleaded. Her pulse was racing. She felt sick. "Just tell me what he's done. I have to know, okay? I've . . . I've been away for a long time."

The boy hesitated. He chewed his lip for a moment, his eyes narrowing. "You really don't know, do you? You don't know *anything?*"

Ariel shook her head furiously. For a moment she forgot about the grasshoppers, her exhaustion—all of it. "You gotta tell me," she insisted. *"Now."*

"Okay, okay." He lowered his eyes. "It's hard to explain. Trevor turned that campus into . . . I don't know, a prison. He watches everybody all the time. He has these labs, and he does experiments." The boy's voice shook. "He's captured all these Visionaries, and he keeps us locked up until we die—"

"Wait, slow down," Ariel interrupted. "Visionaries?"

He nodded, glancing back up at her. "Yeah. People who come for the Chosen One. He doesn't let us fulfill our visions."

Fulfill our visions. Ariel shuddered. So this kid was one of those Chosen One wackos. But why

28

did Trevor even care? What was he doing to them?

"Look, I have to go," the boy muttered. He backed away from her. "That's why I broke out. The security's down. All the locusts are messing up the system. I have to find the Chosen One. She's coming. I saw it again last night. If I'm late, I'm gonna . . . I'm gonna get the plague. I know it. I have to tell her not to come here because the Demon will—"

"No, no," Ariel interrupted. She grabbed him by the shoulders. "Please, you gotta stay and help me. The Chosen One doesn't exist. But if—"

"Don't *say* that!" The boy wrenched free from her grasp and staggered away from her. "Don't you get it? The Chosen One is the only one who can help—"

He broke off, frowning.

His skin flushed. He stared at her—and one of his cheeks grew dark. Black. Gooey.

No! Ariel shook her head, gasping. *Not now!*

The boy's entire face exploded in a shower of blood and pus. Ariel recoiled from him, shielding her eyes with her hands. Her mind went blank. The situation was simply too horrifying.

"I don't believe it," Caleb whispered.

Even after several seconds Ariel was still panting. Her lungs heaved. She couldn't seem to get enough oxygen. All she could think was this: *That boy would have been lucky to get shot.* But she forced herself to open her eyes.

Her throat caught.

The boy's clothes lay in a puddle of black glop, amidst a pack of crawling insects.

"What are we gonna do?" Caleb murmured.

29

Ariel clenched her fists, struggling to regain some self-control. She took a deep breath, then another.

Very gradually her mind began to clear. It was obvious what they were going to do.

They were going to stop Trevor. Period. The world was way too screwed up already for him to be locking people away and doing God-knows-what. *Way* too screwed up. All she had to do was look at the gory remains of that deranged kid to be reminded of *that*. So she was going to give Trevor a piece of her mind—just the way Brian had wanted. She was going to do it for him, for her dead father, for this dead kid, for *everybody*.

"We're gonna rush that place and set Trevor straight," she stated. "We're gonna put an end to whatever's going on there."

"What about the guns?" Caleb asked.

"There's twenty-two of us and one of him," she pointed out. "We'll deal."

"Are . . . are you sure that's so smart?" Caleb stammered.

She shrugged. "Probably not. But you know what? At this point, I really don't care."

FOUR

Amarillo,
Texas
Night of May 10

"Quiet down!" Dr. Harold Wurf commanded. "All of you, quiet down! Now!"

Nobody in the enormous candlelit barn seemed to hear him. Every single one of them was jabbering at once. In their identical white robes, they almost looked like pawns on an overcrowded chessboard. Yes. And he was their king. So why wouldn't they shut up? Hundreds of voices filled the air, complaining and arguing. . . . The sheer volume was unbearable. Harold couldn't *think*. Never before had his entire flock been so unruly—not even in the early days, when so many of them still doubted his powers.

"Listen to me!" he barked.

Once again his words were lost in the cacophony.

Dammit. He was starting to get nervous. He almost wished he had a blast of MDMA or some other stimulant—and he hadn't felt that way in a very, very long time. He was the Healer, the Messiah, the Chosen One. Until last week he'd been impervious to misfortune. He'd reaped the rewards of a dozen miracles. Every disaster brought a sweeter triumph. He'd crushed every nonbeliever; he'd purged his flock of every vice; he'd turned his former home into a paradise.

So why was he being cursed with locusts?

Locusts! Eight days ago they appeared as if by magic—descending upon his vast acres of corn and decimating the crop within hours. The whole predicament was absurdly *biblical.* They turned up everywhere: in his bed, in his food, in his clothing. The only place they avoided was the barn. The candles seemed to repel them. But how long would that last? Would they storm this place as soon as the last flame died out?

Harold ran a hand through his wild mane of dark hair. *Maybe I'm being punished for hubris,* he thought, surveying the crowd. *Maybe I've been too selfish, too full of myself, too hard on the flock. Could it be that I've lost my powers? Could it be—*

"How ya gonna feed us *now,* Harold?" somebody bellowed.

The question cut through the noise.

Finally the room began to quiet down.

"There's no more food! The corn is gone! You screwed up!"

Harold's ice blue eyes burned. He recognized the voice even before he zeroed in on the mop of blond hair and black leather jacket. *George Porter.* Who else? The sniveling little wiseass was easy to spot—an ugly stain amidst the sea of white robes. George still refused to wear the clothing of the Promised Land. He probably thought he was making some sort of dramatic statement. Nobody cared, of course. He was a fool. Yet somehow *he* managed to capture the attention of the flock, whereas Harold could not. It was infuriating.

"How dare you talk to me that way," Harold growled.

George sneered. "Sorry, man. It's just that I have a hard time being polite when I'm starving to death."

Starving to death? Harold almost laughed. Why did teenagers feel the need to exaggerate everything, to dramatize their otherwise banal lives? George had one less ration of corn per day. The quantity was still more than sufficient. Besides, Harold had enough grain and dried vegetables stockpiled to last another . . . well, at least another week.

"So what's your plan?" George demanded. "We're waiting. We all want to know—"

"Why don't you let the Healer speak?" George's girlfriend interrupted. "If you closed your mouth, maybe you'd get an answer."

The entire barn fell completely silent.

A multitude of angry eyes turned to George.

Harold smirked. *Thank you, Julia.* He could kiss her for that. Of course, he could also do a lot more. She looked so pure and innocent—a delicate, thin flower—the way her smooth brown skin contrasted with the white robe, the way her long brown curls cascaded over her shoulders. Innocent . . . but sexy, too. Yes, yes. Anger did wonders for her soft eyes. What did she see in George, anyway? He truly *was* like a stain. A stain that should probably be wiped clean. Then Harold could have sweet Julia Morrison all to himself. . . .

Uh-oh.

He was getting distracted.

The flock was staring at him again, waiting for a response.

"*I* have an answer," a girl with a British accent suddenly announced from the back of the barn.

People shifted in their chairs.

"I've seen it in a vision. It came to me last night."

Harold's smile widened. Well, well. Just in time. Young women really came through for him, didn't they? First Julia—and now Linda Altman, this new arrival, this mysterious girl from England. She, too, was beautiful. She looked a lot like his old friend Larissa, in fact: blond, blue-eyed, and well endowed. Of course, he had yet to find out if Linda was like Larissa in other ways . . . specifically, if she was promiscuous and willing. But he would find out. He would make it a priority.

"And what was this vision?" Harold called.

Linda stood and smiled back at him. "I saw *you*. And I saw all of us, everybody here, praying inside this barn at night. And as we prayed, you grew as tall as the silo outside. Then you swept your hand over the farm, and the locusts vanished." Her smile faltered for a moment. "But . . . but . . ."

"Go on," Harold pressed.

She shook her head gravely. "I also saw the Demon. And I know that the Demon is strong."

Harold blinked a few times. *The Demon.*

If someone had said the word *demon* six months ago, he probably would have had that person institutionalized. Even as recently as April, he would have shrugged the notion off with a disdainful laugh. But in the wake of everything he'd learned—about the

34

Visionaries, about *himself*—he couldn't be so quick to judge. If he were truly the Chosen One, then what was so implausible about the existence of a Demon?

"What else?" he asked.

Linda glanced around the barn, shifting on her feet. She seemed anxious, preoccupied. "The Demon is strong because *we're* weak," she stated quietly.

Harold frowned. "What do you mean?"

"There are people here who don't follow the Seven Commandments." Her eyes flashed to George. "There are people here who—"

"What the hell are you looking at *me* for?" George shouted. He laughed harshly. "I'm not the only one. Do you know how hard it is to follow those rules? One of them says we aren't supposed to have sex. That isn't natural, Linda. That—"

"Silence!" Harold barked. "Let the girl finish!"

George rolled his eyes.

"What I'm trying to tell you is that we all need to be stronger," Linda pleaded. Her voice took on a sense of urgency. "The Demon brought this plague upon us. We've become corrupted. Not all of us are pure. We need to follow the rule of the Healer—not only in our deeds, but in our hearts and souls as well."

George let loose with another obnoxious laugh. "Jesus, Linda, *listen* to yourself. Hearts and souls? You sound like Dial-A-Prayer. Do you honestly think the Demon gives a crap about what we think or believe? I know the Demon, too. And I know—"

"That's *enough!*" Harold shouted. The veins bulged in his neck. Fury swelled inside him once again. So.

Linda's visions revealed the truth: Heretics like George were destroying his paradise, his Promised Land. It was an outrage. He jerked a finger at George. "*You* brought this plague upon us!"

George didn't answer. He glared back at Harold, then pushed himself out of his chair. It scraped against the barn floor with a painful screech. He began shoving his way toward the door. Julia rushed after him.

"Wait, George—stop!" Linda cried. She turned back to Harold, her face creased with fear. "It's not just George. It's all of us. None of us are pure. And all of us need to repent if we're going to stop the Demon. Don't you see? That was part of my vision, too. We need to stay in this barn tonight and pray. *All* of us."

Harold raised his eyebrows.

"That's up to George," he stated as calmly as he could.

George froze in his tracks. He shot a cold stare at Harold, then glanced at Julia. She was whispering feverishly to him . . . but Harold was too far away to hear her words. Still, it didn't take a genius like Harold to surmise what she was saying. She was clearly begging George to sit down. She clearly believed what Linda and everybody else in this barn believed: that if George continued to act like an immature child, then they would have no chance at expelling the locusts.

"All right, fine," George grumbled loudly. He forced his way back through the crowd and flopped into his chair. "Whatever. I can kick it in the barn for one night. But these bugs *better* be gone when I wake up."

"They will, George," Linda soothed. She smiled reverently at Harold. "I know it."

I know it, too, Harold thought. And it was true. The feelings of uncertainty had all but faded. How could he ever doubt his own powers? After all, he had the power to influence weak little kids like George Porter, didn't he? He chuckled to himself. Of course, that was easy. That didn't take any supernatural gift. No . . . his true power lay in the fact that this girl, this perfect *stranger,* had seen him in a vision.

His true power lay in the miracles he performed and would continue to perform—again and again and again.

And tonight would be no exception.

PART II:

May 11–May 21

**Amarillo,
Texas
Morning of May 11**

My baby is growing.

Every day she looks more like me. I see it in her eyes.

But she's scared. She's crying, wailing away at the edge of the cliff . . . and there's nothing I can do. The moon is very bright. The Demon is out. So are her helpers. The Demon never acts alone. I know my baby feels their presence, too. Every time the Demon or her helpers come near—

Somebody shook George's arm.

He rolled over, scowling. What was the big idea? He needed to *sleep.*

"George, wake up!" Julia whispered. "You have to see this!"

Later, he thought. But he was too tired to actually form the word. He couldn't even open his eyes. Man, was he groggy. Where the hell was he, anyway? His mind was in serious haze. Wherever he was, it wasn't comfortable. He was lying on something really hard. The floor? Maybe. He wrinkled his nose. It smelled kind of funky here, too—

"George!" Julia yelled. "Wake up!"

Ow! Her voice exploded in his brain. Why was she shouting? His head was *pounding* all of a sudden. He licked his lips. They tasted like stale sandpaper. His mouth was so dry. . . . *Hold up*. He knew this feeling. Of course he did. It was a monster hangover. Did he get drunk last night? He couldn't remember a thing.

Julia shook him again—a little more roughly this time.

Finally his eyelids fluttered open. His vision was blurred . . . but he could see Julia's face hovering over him, fuzzy and ill defined. "What's going on?" he croaked. "What's the matter?"

"It's a miracle, George," she whispered. "Just like they said. The locusts are dead!"

Locusts. Yeah . . . now he remembered. He was in Harold's barn. That was where the stink was coming from. And he'd spent all night sitting around, bored out of his skull, while everybody else prayed for forgiveness. They actually *prayed*. Even his girlfriend . . . He sat up and shook his head, blinking in the sunlight that streamed through cracks in the ceiling. Well, at least he knew he couldn't be hung over. Booze wasn't allowed on the premises. It was one of those stupid Seven Commandments.

So why did he feel like such crap?

"Come out and see," Julia insisted, taking his hand. "It's incredible."

But George couldn't quite move yet. He blinked at her a few times. Now that the blurriness had faded, he could see that Julia didn't look as hot as usual. She was still beautiful, of course—but there were dark sacks under her soft brown eyes. And her face seemed bloated. *She* looked hung over, too.

"Uh . . . can I ask you something?" he mumbled.

She nodded absently, staring at the barn door. "Of course."

"How do you feel?"

She laughed. "Not so great, actually. I threw up this morning."

"You did?" That was weird, wasn't it? *He* was sick, and *she* was sick. . . . He glanced around the barn. It was almost empty, except for a few stragglers who were stumbling toward the door in their white robes. *They* looked a little out of it, too. "Did we, like, eat some bad corn or something last night?"

She turned and flashed him a puzzled smile. "No, George."

He frowned.

"All we had was water, remember?" she added.

"Right, right," he muttered. "Harold didn't put whiskey in it or anything, did he?"

"Whiskey?" She laughed again and cocked her eyebrow. "I think I probably would have noticed. I *know* you would have."

George forced a tired grin. "I guess. I just don't know why I feel so lousy. . . ."

"Don't worry about it." Julia tugged at his hand and stood up. "Come on."

He nodded, but he still felt distracted and agitated. Something wasn't right. But he'd probably feel better soon enough. Maybe he was just coming down with a fever or something. He forced himself to his feet. His legs wobbled.

"Hey," Julia murmured, wrapping her arm around him. "Are you okay?"

"Just a little dizzy." He gave her a quick, reassuring squeeze. "I'm fine. But I—"

Before he'd even finished, she was dragging him across the straw-covered floor and out into the sunshine. The bright glare practically blinded him. What was so important, anyway? Everybody was in the fields, laughing and dancing and yelling like a bunch of nutcases . . . and there was something in the air. George sniffed. His eyes narrowed. *Damn.* The funk out *here* was about a hundred times worse than in the barn. It didn't smell like poop, either. It had a rank, acidic edge—like cleaning spray or something.

"See what I mean?" Julia cried. She let go of his arm and waved her hands at the fields. "The bugs are all dead! All of them! We can start planting again!"

Blecch. George stuck out his tongue. Harold had obviously used some kind of serious industrial-strength poison to get rid of the locusts. Only he'd been a little too late. The so-called Promised Land was a dust bowl. George squinted at the mob of kids, kicking up dirt and raising a hoopla in the middle of the rows and rows of barren cornstalks. They looked like jerks. He could hear their feet crunching on the remains of the bugs. What were they so happy about? Harold should have sprayed this place *days* ago. Then there might be some corn left. Would anything even grow here again?

"What's wrong?" Julia asked.

"That stink, for one," he muttered. "Do you think it's safe to breathe?"

"Of *course* it is!" She giggled. "Why wouldn't it be?"

He shrugged. "I don't know. Maybe we should let this chemical stuff settle in before we start messing

42

around in the fields. Maybe that's what's making us feel so ill."

Julia stared at him. "What chemical stuff?"

"Whatever Harold used to kill all the bugs." He took another whiff. "I mean, don't you think it's nasty?"

"George . . . you're not making any sense." Julia's brow grew furrowed. "Harold didn't use any stuff. *We* killed the bugs."

"Yeah, right." He snickered. "How come I don't remember calling the exterminator?"

"We killed them with our prayers," she said.

Our prayers. George hesitated. He looked deep into Julia's eyes, searching for a trace of humor, a sparkle—anything. But she wasn't laughing. She looked nervous.

"Don't you remember last night?" Julia asked.

He took a step back from her. All right. This was a little too weird. They weren't communicating. Was this a joke? No, no—he knew when she was joking. Normally they didn't even have to use words to understand each other. Normally he could read her thoughts with just a glance, just a change of expression. . . .

"What's *wrong*, George?" she pleaded.

"You tell me," he said cautiously. "I mean, can't you smell it, Julia? It reeks."

"I *know!*" she cried. She laughed—but there was a desperate edge in her voice. "It smells like dead locusts. There are *millions* of them, George. What do you expect? It's not going to smell like perfume."

George's breath came faster. "Listen, Julia, I don't know what you're thinking—but dead bugs do *not*

43

smell like this. Chemicals smell like this. Bug spray smells . . ." He didn't finish. A sickening idea began to dawn on him. "Wait. Who told you how the locusts died?"

"Nobody," Julia stated. Her smile faded. "I walked out here and saw it for myself. And I heard people talking. I heard them talking about the Healer's miracle."

Oh, brother. Now *he* was starting to feel queasy. The Healer? Why did she have to call him that? His name was Harold. She wasn't turning into one of his brainwashed bozos, was she? She *was* wearing that stupid robe . . . but no. No way. Not Julia. She was much too smart for that. George *knew* her—as well as he knew himself. She was a Visionary. . . .

"Hey, guys!"

Linda Altman came running toward them out of the fields, her blond hair and white robe fluttering in the wind. "Isn't it amazing—"

"Linda, you're sharp," George interrupted, looking her straight in the face. "Now tell me something. What's that smell?"

She stopped in front of him and smirked. "Is this a trick question?" she asked, glancing at Julia.

"No." He shook his head. "Just tell me. What is it?"

"It smells like dead bugs to me, George," Linda replied without batting an eyelash. There was a mild sarcastic undertone in her voice, as if she were talking to a little kid—or a chump. "How's that for an answer?"

"Dead bugs," he repeated. Had the whole world gone crazy? "Well, I don't buy it. I think Harold sprayed the fields last night while we were sleeping."

Julia sighed. "George, I don't understand—"

"I was talking to Linda," he snapped. The words came out of his mouth before he could stop them.

Neither Julia nor Linda uttered a peep. Linda swallowed and looked nervous. Julia's brown eyes filled with tears.

Time seemed to stand still.

And then Julia stormed away from him—out toward the field.

"Julia, wait!" George cried. He pushed past Linda and dashed after his girlfriend, lunging to grab her arm. What the hell was happening to him? He'd never been mean to her before. He felt sick, ashamed . . . but mostly he felt *scared*. He didn't understand what was going on with her—and it was making him crazy.

"Look, I—I'm sorry," he stammered. "I just—I don't know what's up with you. It's like you're blind or something."

She shook free of his grip. *"I'm* blind?" she shrieked. "Then how come *you're* the only one who can't see the truth?" Her face softened for a moment. "What's this about, George? I mean, really. What's this about?"

George opened his mouth, but no words would come. He couldn't believe it. He and Julia were actually fighting. It just didn't seem possible. He *loved* her. But why had she changed so much? What had gotten into her? His heart bounced in his chest. They hadn't even kissed in over three weeks. He should have never let her talk him into staying in this freakish place. He should have gotten her out of here and kept going west. . . .

"I think maybe you're jealous of Harold," she whispered tremulously. "But—"

"Jealous?" he cried. A momentary pang of anger flashed through him. "You gotta be *kidding* me! He's a punk, Julia, just like me—a scammer. The only difference is that he's a whole lot smarter and luckier. But he's still a punk."

Julia's face fell. "How can you say that?" she cried. "How can you . . ."

She suddenly clamped her mouth shut.

Her eyes shifted to something over George's shoulder. A strained smile appeared on her lips.

"I made good on my promise, didn't I, George?" a deep voice asked.

Harold. George whirled around. He *hated* the way Harold was always sneaking up on people. The jerk was standing there in his white lab coat, his brown hair pulled back in a ponytail. Funny: *His* face was all puffy, too. He wasn't so godly that the poison didn't screw him up. He was just like everyone else. But he looked so damn full of himself—with his hands folded across his chest and that smug smile. . . .

"I made good on my promise," Harold repeated. "The bugs are gone."

George shook his head. "How'd you do it, Harold? I mean, what did you use?"

Harold raised his eyebrows. "What did I use?"

"Why don't you just admit how you did it?" George yelled. "I mean, what's the big deal? You still *killed* them. It's not like anybody here is gonna dis you for it. I just want to know."

"You want to know *what?*" Harold asked, glancing at Julia and Linda. "I don't understand." He didn't sound angry or upset—just puzzled.

46

"George thinks you sprayed the fields with chemicals while we were sleeping last night," Julia muttered. She lowered her head, as if she'd never been more embarrassed in her life.

Harold chuckled lightly. "George, if I had insecticides, don't you think I would have used them a long time ago? Think about it. It doesn't make any sense. The corn is gone. Why wouldn't I have tried to save it?"

"I don't know why," George shot back. "But there's some kind of heavy-duty poison out here—and it's clogging up my nostrils and making us all sick. So don't try to lay your bull on me. It's not gonna fly."

"I'm not trying to fool you, George," Harold stated. His voice was calm. "You're too smart for that. I can't explain the odor . . . other than that our prayers were answered. But I can tell you this: The smell of death isn't pleasant. Believe me, I know. And there's a lot of death here—millions and millions of locusts. I didn't spray the fields. I prayed in the barn with you until I fell asleep. I dreamed I saw the locusts die, and they did. That's the truth."

George almost laughed. That was the best Harold could do? A dream? No, that wasn't good enough. Not at all. *George* was the Visionary—not Harold.

"What about my vision, George?" Linda murmured. "I *saw* what happened. I knew that if we all stayed in the barn and prayed, the Demon would be defeated. The plague would lift. And it did."

"Yeah, but you know what? I didn't pray." George's voice hardened. "I mean, didn't you say that *all* of us had to pray? With pure hearts or whatever? My heart wasn't pure. No freaking way." He glowered at Harold. "And another thing. *I* had a dream, too. Just before I woke up. And I saw the Demon. It wasn't defeated. It was stronger than ever—"

"George, *please!*" Julia wailed. "Just stop it! Just—just . . ." She didn't finish. All at once she bolted back into the barn.

George stood still for a moment, unable to do anything but watch. His heart squeezed. He was suddenly paralyzed with fear, with remorse. His rage vanished. Was he losing her? Was he really *losing* her? It couldn't be possible.

"Julia!" he shouted. "No! I'm sorry! Come back. . . ."

But she was gone.

Harold gave a disappointed sigh. "Look what you've done now, George. What do you want me to say? Obviously the prayers made a difference, regardless of what you did. Your girlfriend certainly thinks so. And as for your dream . . . maybe you should look inside yourself. Maybe the Demon has a stronger hold on you than you think."

George's jaw tightened. Harold had *no* business talking to him like that. Harold didn't know a damn thing about the Demon or the Chosen One. He just pretended that he did. It was a front—like everything else. And the game he was playing had gone too far. It had put up a wall between George and Julia . . . a wall that separated George from the only person he had ever truly loved.

But that was it. No more. George wasn't going to let Harold ruin the one good thing in his life. He was going to smash that wall to bits.

"I'm gonna get you," George spat. His voice

quavered. "You're not the Chosen One. This whole thing is a sham. I'm gonna prove how you killed the locusts. I'm gonna show everyone what a goddamn fake you are. I'm gonna do it for Julia."

Harold just smiled. "Go ahead and try, George." He hesitated, then leaned forward and patted George's shoulder. "In the past, I probably would have killed you. But the Healer is not violent. So I'm going to let you prove that I'm a fraud. I'm going to give you the run of the Promised Land so you can search for evidence against me. I think that's a more fitting punishment. Because you won't find a thing. You'll only end up believing in me."

CHAPTER
SIX

Splicing wires was not Trevor's forte . . . especially at night, with only the light of the moon to guide him. No, even under the best of circumstances, he was no repairman. His talents lay in design. In *planning*. With the right tools and material he could direct a thousand men to rewire an entire city. But sadly enough, he lacked the basic skills of an *electrician*—the lowliest henchman in the engineering hierarchy. And at this point he had no choice but to make do with what little ability he had.

"Get me some more of that roach killer," he ordered.

Barney nodded. "I'll see if we have any left." He dashed across the lawn and disappeared into the communications lab.

Trevor sighed. It was hopeless. He'd been working on this ruined fuse box for hours, fumbling in the dark with a soldering iron in a vain effort to patch the chewed wires back together. And he'd accomplished nothing. Over half the television monitors were still dead. Every single one of his friends was working in a different location, feverishly trying to mend what they could, while others attempted to stave off further destruction by wrapping the few remaining unscathed cables in layers and layers of electric tape. But the locusts were simply too numerous. A bottle of roach killer was effective for neutralizing them in a small area for a brief amount of time . . . but they always returned.

Is there a queen? he wondered, collapsing back into the cool grass. *If we kill the queen, we can stop them from reproducing. . . .*

No. Such a task would be virtually impossible. It would mean singling out one insect among millions. For a moment he gazed up at the cloudless, starry sky—until several locusts flew into his face, squirming over his mouth and nostrils. *Jeez!* He bolted back upright, sputtering, furiously slapping at his own cheeks.

The gnawing fear within him began to grow.

He was never going to find a solution, was he?

He was suddenly certain of it. The bugs were going to keep reproducing and eating away at everything until nothing remained. Trevor's pulse quickened. His reign over this place was over. He'd never find a cure for the melting plague or Chosen One syndrome. Whatever mysterious phenomenon had caused those diseases must have also done something to the immune systems of locusts. He could think of no other reasonable explanation. Insects were supposed to dominate the earth after a nuclear war, right? So why wouldn't they dominate the earth after some *other* kind of catastrophe—

"Jezebel's loose!"

Trevor whirled around.

Barney was standing in the open doorway of the communications lab, holding his rifle, his flaccid jowls quivering.

"I thought you put a guard outside her door after the power failure," Trevor said. "Are you telling me she got away *again*?"

"She locked herself in the command center!" Barney cried. "She won't come out!"

Holy . . .

Trevor tried to push himself to his feet, but his legs seemed unstable. The locusts vanished from his thoughts. If Jezebel had locked herself inside the command center, then there was no way to get to her. She could wreak whatever havoc she wanted. The room was stocked with rifles. Within seconds she could destroy what was left of the surveillance system—four months' worth of work. *No!* He stumbled across the lawn and shoved Barney aside.

"I—I don't know how it happened," Barney stammered. "She managed to pick the lock or something and . . ."

But Trevor was already thundering down the dark corridor. He rounded the corner and threw himself against the closed door of the command center at full speed. His body slammed against the cold metal—but nothing happened, of course. All he managed to do was bruise himself. No, it would take several pounds of dynamite to blast into that room. He'd overseen the reinforcement of the hinges and frame himself. His heart thumped. Why was she doing this? What did she *want?*

"Who is it?" Jezebel called teasingly.

"It's me," Trevor gasped, pressing his ear against the door. "What's going on, Jez?"

"Not much," she answered. Her disembodied voice seemed very far away. "I just got bored. I wanted to watch some tube. I gotta say, this room is pretty swank. I mean, in a totally wacked way. It's like *1984* or something. Did you read that book? I did, last semester. Well, I only read the Cliffs Notes, but—"

"Jez, listen to me," he pleaded, fighting to keep the panic out of his voice. "I want you to let me in so we can talk, all right? Just the two of us. How does that sound?"

She laughed. "To be honest, Trev, that sounds pretty lame."

Damn. He chewed his lip for a second. "What about us?" he asked. His voice grew tender. "I thought we were happy together."

"Happy together," she repeated flatly. "Trevor, you locked me in a cell. It's sort of hard to keep up a relationship under those conditions. Plus you *know* that the only reason I slept with you was so that I'd have a place to crash. You repulse me."

Rage flashed through him. *That bitch!* After everything he'd done for her . . . but no, he couldn't let himself get angry. She was obviously suffering a profound mental breakdown. *This isn't the real Jezebel,* he reminded himself.

"Psst!" Barney whispered over Trevor's shoulder. "I think I got a solution. We can get in there through the air-conditioning duct."

Trevor hesitated. *Yes.* But if they tried to sneak up on her through the vents, she'd definitely hear them.

And they'd be easy targets. She had guns. Lives would probably be lost. He shook his head and waved Barney away. No—they would only use that option as a last resort. They had to coax her out on her own terms.

"Hey, if you're thinking about getting to me through the air-conditioning vent, you can forget about it," she remarked nonchalantly. "I'd blow you away."

Trevor's blood ran cold.

"Anyway, you're smarter than that, Trev," she added. "That's so, like . . . hackneyed. I mean, how many action movies end with a guy sneaking through the *vent?* A lot."

He shot a quick, horrified glance at Barney. Barney's pale skin looked almost green. He backed away from the door—then turned, bolted down the hall, and clattered up the stairs. But Trevor wasn't angry. No. *He* wanted to run, too. After a few seconds he took a deep breath. "So what do you want, Jez?"

"What do you *think* I want?" she snapped. "I want you to let me go."

"You, uh . . . you seemed to have taken care of that yourself," he stammered.

She laughed again. "I guess you're right. But thing is, I just know that you're gonna come after me. And there's a very simple reason for that. You're desperate to get laid."

His face reddened. "Shut up!" he barked. "You don't—"

"But that's not all," she interrupted. "The other reason is that you don't *listen* very well. Like when I warned you before that you would suffer the consequences. Didn't I say that? Yes. But did you listen?

Noooo. Now look at you. This place is a mess. Look at all these bugs."

Trevor snorted, now more contemptuous than afraid. "Are you telling me that *you* sent the locusts? Is that what you're saying? That's insane!"

"Spare me." She groaned. "Of course I didn't send the locusts. Let's just say that I knew something bad was gonna happen. And I gave you some advance warning. Just like I'm doing right now."

He blinked. His sneer faded. "What do you mean?"

"Go up to the second-floor window and see for yourself, okay?" she answered casually. "I'll wait here. But get ready. It's gonna be a *big* shocker."

Trevor swallowed hard.

"Go on," she commanded. "I can see everything just fine from this TV set."

His eyes flashed down the corridor. The stairwell was shrouded in darkness. Was she bluffing? Or did she have an uncanny ability to foretell the future? *No, no, no!* Of course she didn't! She was a psychotic. She was prone to fits of paranoid babbling. All that other stuff was just coincidence. Now he was losing his mind.

"Trevor!" Barney's voice reverberated down the stairwell. "Get up here!"

The color drained from Trevor's face.

"You better go, Trev!" Jezebel shouted delightedly.

Just coincidence, he repeated to himself. But he knew he didn't believe it. He sprinted down the hall and hurtled up the steps. Barney waited for him at the top, clutching a rifle in either hand. Trevor grabbed one from him and hurried toward the window—where several more of his friends were crouched, rifles drawn.

"What's up?" he asked as calmly as he could.

"We got visitors," one of them answered.

Trevor leaned forward and peered through the glass. There must have been twenty kids out on the lawn—and they were all carrying torches. *The gate!* He glanced over at the barbed wire fence. A huge hole had been cut right into the front of it—a makeshift door. But how? When? Had they been so preoccupied with *fixing* the security that they'd forgotten about it altogether?

"I don't think they're armed," another stated. "I don't see any guns."

Trevor nodded distractedly. Then he frowned.

Wait a minute.

Where were all the locusts? They seemed to have disappeared—at least in the immediate area. Did the flames keep them away?

"What do you want to do?" Barney asked.

"I don't know," Trevor murmured. "Have they said anything?"

Everyone shook their heads at once.

Interesting. Trevor cocked the rifle. Remarkably, he was starting to relax a little. Yes, the absence of locusts was *very* interesting, to say the least. The torches must be responsible for scaring them away. That meant he knew how to deal with them. Some carefully placed bonfires would rid his compound of the bugs forever.

A grin curled on his lips. He almost felt as if he should thank these kids. He surveyed the rabble carefully, seeking out any weapons—but there were none. They couldn't pose much of a threat. So much for Jezebel's dire predictions.

"I'll fire a warning shot," he said after a moment. "If that doesn't scare them off, then we'll take a few of them out. We'll each pick a target. Just boys. Don't shoot any girls. That ought to send the rest of them running."

"Good idea," Barney agreed.

The others nodded. Trevor reached out and opened the window—just a crack. He slid the barrel of his rifle through the opening. But before he could pull the trigger, a slender girl with long hair stepped forward.

"Trevor?" she called. "Trevor, is that you?"

He gasped. *That voice!*

The gun almost slipped from his fingers. He staggered back a few steps, shaking his head. Was it *her?* But how? Never once did it occur to him that *she* would come back here. Not after what he did. . . .

"Trevor?" Barney asked worriedly. "Who is that?"

But Trevor couldn't speak. He could only stare down at . . . the girl. There was no doubt anymore as to who she was. His insides twisted in a painful knot. Even though her hair was longer and her face was obscured by shadow, he still knew. The shape of her body, the way she half slouched when she stood, even that cocky tone of voice—all of it was as familiar as his own reflection.

"It's my little sister," he finally croaked.

"Ariel?" Barney cried. "But I thought you said she split town for good."

He shook his head again. "That's what I thought—"

"Trevor!" Ariel yelled again. She waved her torch at the window. "Stop being a wuss and come out here! We gotta talk!"

Wuss? His grip tightened on the gun.

"What are you scared of?" she taunted. "You scared I'm gonna make you look like the loser you are in front of all your geek buddies?" She hesitated, then glanced back at the crowd. "Actually—forget the talk. You'd just bore the hell out of me, anyway. I think I'm gonna go ahead and burn this place right down."

She hurled her torch at one of the doors. It bounced and fell to the dried grass, still burning.

One of Trevor's friends glanced over his shoulder and frowned at him. "You still want to fire that warning shot?" he asked.

Trevor didn't answer. For some strange reason, one thought kept whirling through his mind: *Jezebel.* She was right again. She'd warned him that a big shock was coming. A *bad* shock. He no longer doubted her psychic gifts. Not at all. This *was* bad. Ariel was here for one reason—and it wasn't to mend their broken bond. Of course not. She'd come here for a fight.

If that was what she wanted, that was what she would get.

He'd show her just how much of a wuss he was.

Ah, yes . . . but he wouldn't harm her. No. She could be of use to him. Especially when it came to Jezebel. After all, she still knew Jezebel better than anybody else. Better than *he* did, certainly. They were friends. She might have some valuable insights into

Jezebel's . . . *condition*. She might know if Jezebel had always been crazy, or lucky, or gifted with an ability to tell the future.

And if she didn't, well—

"Trevor!" one of the boys barked. "What do you want us to do?"

"Screw the warning shot," he breathed. "They're trespassing. Shoot them."

His friends hesitated. They exchanged nervous glances. "But—"

"Everyone except Ariel," Trevor finished. "I want her alive."

Upon that final order, he smashed the window with the butt of his rifle, flipped it in his arms, and pulled the trigger on the torch-bearing mob. His friends followed suit. It happened very quickly. He couldn't see much through the barrage of bullets . . . but in less than a minute, nobody was left standing on the front lawn except his little sister.

He was breathing very heavily.

Everyone else was either dead or gone.

SEVEN

Night of May 14
Cruise Ship *The Majestic*,
Somewhere in the North Atlantic

". . . combining rich maple syrup and hearty granola!" a woman's voice crackled from the small radio. "One bite and you'll—"

The voice was lost in static. Sarah frowned. *Come on,* she silently urged. She carefully twisted the dial in either direction.

". . . Crunch-errific!" the voice squawked.

Sarah froze. She held her breath.

"Now *dat's* what I'm tawkin' about," a guy with a phony Brooklyn accent added. "When I tawk breakfast, I wanna . . ."

Static filled the speaker again. *Damn!* Sarah fiddled with the dial—a little more frantically this time. There were a few incoherent mutterings, some sappy music, then the announcement faded completely in a hiss of white noise.

Still—she'd heard enough, hadn't she?

Yes. Yes, she had. A tingle of excitement raced up her spine.

America is plague-free.

It had to be. Because the only people who would broadcast such a stupid commercial were adults. Yes.

Civilized, responsible adults. Who else would bother? *Teenagers* certainly wouldn't try to peddle some foul breakfast food, especially in the middle of an apocalypse. Besides, advertising required certain conditions, certain *adult* conditions; namely, a good economy, a stable government—but most of all, a willingness to waste time and resources on something ridiculous.

So the soldiers were right. Those few tantalizing scraps of garbage proved it. America hadn't changed one bit. *Hot damn!* Sarah flipped the radio off and slumped into the plush, velvet chair. She felt like singing.

For the first time ever, she could actually relax. She could enjoy the fact that she was steaming back home on a luxury liner—that she was no longer a prisoner, no longer starving, no longer filthy. She could sit back and revel in her new surroundings: a first-class cabin with a king-sized bed.

She could enjoy *life* again.

Now she was certain that her parents had survived. She reached across the antique mahogany desk and snatched up her journal.

Finally confirmed the rumors about America. Big relief, because The Majestic is headed for New York, per my instructions. The soldiers say that we ought to be docking in just over two weeks. They

*have to sail slowly in order
to conserve fuel. They keep
apologizing to me because they
can't get there any faster. I
don't mind, but they're
clearly afraid of me.*

Sarah paused for a moment. The soldiers really
were afraid of her, weren't they? Everybody on board
was—even the kids whom she'd saved from the lottery. Nobody looked her in the eyes anymore . . . nobody except Ibrahim. People avoided her when she
walked around the ship. They either stopped in their
tracks or hurried in the opposite direction.

Now that she thought about it, she was actually
pretty lonely.

Oh, well. A brief spell of loneliness was a small
price to pay for coming home. She hunched back
over the desk.

*Fear can be a good tool,
though. Fear ended the lottery.
I even convinced the soldiers
to pick up more passengers.
We stopped at Tangier to
scavenge for food and medical
supplies. We found lots of
kids who were desperate to
leave, so we brought them all*

*on board. People are sleeping
in the halls. But everybody
has enough to eat. I'm proud
of what I*

There was a knock on the door.

"Who is it?" Sarah called.

"Ibrahim," came the soft reply.

"Hey!" she cried. She slammed the notebook shut and hopped out of her chair. "Come in, come in!" She flung open the door. "I have great news!"

He smiled eagerly. "Did you crack the code?" he asked, stepping inside.

The code?

Her excitement abruptly faded.

No, she hadn't cracked the code. She hadn't even *thought* of the code embedded in the text of the scroll . . . not since the day that unbeliever melted. She hadn't looked at the prophecies, either. Not once. The scroll lay on the night table by the side of her bed—untouched and unread, like a discarded book.

"You *are* working on the scroll, aren't you?" Ibrahim asked. His tone was very friendly and casual.

No, Ibrahim. No, I'm not.

Her eyes wandered over to the yellowed parchment. Familiar but long-forgotten feelings of self-loathing began to creep up on her. Why *wasn't* she looking at the scroll? So many mysteries remained; so many people were still in danger. But once again, she had only thought about herself. The scroll had served its purpose by placing her in charge of this ship. *She* was out of danger—at least for the time being. She was on her way to paradise. Looking at the scroll couldn't benefit her any more than it already had. And when they got to the States, she'd figured, the adults would take care of everything . . . as if somehow these ancient prophecies that had destroyed the entire world would just go away once the scroll reached America. As if somehow she was off the hook.

Some Chosen One I am, she thought bitterly.

"Well . . . ah, you can tell me the news later," Ibrahim murmured clumsily. "I just wanted to know what you'd like for supper."

She bowed her head. *Supper.* That summed it up. Oh, yes. She could have anything she wanted. The kids on board would serve the last meal on earth to her on a silver platter if she so desired. Everybody waited on her; everybody was her servant. And why? So she could lounge in this deluxe suite while everyone else slept on the floor? So she could waste her time fooling around with a radio to prove what everybody else already knew? She closed the door and sauntered back to her chair, flopping down at the desk. It was *disgusting*.

Ibrahim cleared his throat. "Sarah? Are you all right? I didn't mean to upset you—"

"No, no, it's not *you*," she gently interrupted. "I'm the one who should be apologizing."

"For what?"

She turned to him. "We're still in trouble, aren't we?"

He hesitated, furrowing his brow. "What do you mean?"

"I mean . . . we're still a long way off from figuring out what's going on."

Ibrahim nodded. "Yes, but you've made so much progress—"

"But what about all the kids who *aren't* going to America? What about the Demon, and the plague, and the False Prophet?" Her voice rose. "What about all that?"

He blinked, clearly baffled. "I—I thought you were trying to solve those riddles," he stammered.

"That's what I should have been doing," she answered glumly. She stared at him. "Can I ask you a question, Ibrahim?"

He nodded emphatically. "Anything."

"Are you scared of me?"

His jaw dropped. *"Scared* of you? What do you mean?"

"I mean . . . I don't know." She paused, frightened of what she was about to say. "Do you look at me differently, now that you know the truth?"

He took a step toward her. "I *always* knew the truth, Sarah," he breathed. "I'm the one who found you. I'm the one who saw you in a vision. I still have those visions. How could I look at you any differently from when I first met you? I knew then what I know now—that you're a divine creature."

"But that's just the thing," she muttered, shaking her head. "I mean, when you first found me, you didn't think I was, like . . . a *savior.*" She stumbled hastily over the word. "You still believed in the hidden Imam and the wrath of Allah and—"

"I made a mistake, Sarah," he stated. He lowered his eyes. "That's all I can say."

She took a deep breath. She felt very confused; she didn't even know why she was so upset anymore. "But what exactly do you see in your visions? How do you know that I'm the Chosen One?"

He looked at her again. "I see your face. I see what I've always seen—first saving you in the desert, then pulling you out of the ocean."

"But how does that prove that I'm the Chosen One?" she pressed. "What does it even mean?"

"Sarah, *you* proved that you're the Chosen One!" he cried. "You proved it with your scroll. You proved it with your prophecies."

She swiveled back to the desk. "Right," she mumbled, staring down at her closed notebook. "The scroll and the prophecies. How could I forget?"

Ibrahim was silent for a moment. "What's bothering you, Sarah?" he finally asked. "Tell me. Please."

"It bothers me that I've *changed*," she said, swallowing. "I'm a totally different person. I used to care about helping people. I used to care about finding out the truth. But now all I care about is myself." Her voice cracked. For a second or two she thought she might cry. "How can I be the Chosen One? I did forget about the scroll . . . and if America is untouched by all these disasters, by all the prophecies, why do we even *need* a Chosen One?"

Ibrahim rushed across the room and swept her up in his arms. *I needed that.* She squeezed him back as tightly as she could, burying her face in his shoulder. Her eyes moistened. It had been so long since she'd actually *touched* another human being. She'd been so isolated. . . .

"It's not true, Sarah," Ibrahim whispered. He gently stroked her long brown hair. "I've never met anyone as selfless as you." He stepped apart from her. "Come on. Let's have a look at the scroll right now. It will make you feel better. You can translate for me."

Sarah nodded, sniffling. She wiped her eyes as he gently lifted the scroll off the night table and sat down on the edge of the vast, unmade bed.

"Come on," he urged. "Sit with me."

"Okay," she murmured. She sank down beside him and took one of the wooden pegs, unraveling a portion of the parchment across both of their laps. Maybe Ibrahim was right. Yes. There was a simple solution to her problem. She needed to start studying the prophecies again. She needed to prepare herself for the uncertainty ahead. She needed to make the most of these two weeks at sea—to devote all of her energy to deciphering the code, to systematically recording and organizing all of her discoveries in her journal. *Then* she would have a shot at redeeming herself. She would arrive in America prepared to explain the importance of the prophecies. Her parents would know who to go to. They'd take Sarah to adults who could make a difference, who could help her figure out how to stop the prophecies, defeat the Demon. . . . There was no point in focusing on her own guilt. It was a waste of time.

"Translate the section about this month," he prodded.

"Okay," she breathed. Her eyes skimmed the lines of Hebrew words until they locked in on the words *Iyar* and *Sivan:* the fifth lunar cycle. For a moment she skimmed down, reading to herself. There was a bit about the False Prophet, then . . .

She paused, frowning.

"Well?" Ibrahim asked.

"I don't know." She shook her head. "It says that the Chosen One will draw closer to the Demon. So I guess the Demon must be in America, right? I mean, it would make sense. We're getting closer to America. I'm pretty sure this False Prophet is there, too." She glanced at him. "There was something about 'the New World' in the part about the last lunar cycle."

He smiled encouragingly. "Go on."

Her eyes fell back to the parchment, back to the top of the passage. "The whole prophecy starts: 'The servants of the Demon will produce miracle after miracle.'"

"Servants of the Demon?"

She nodded, but her mind was drifting. The words triggered a memory—a memory of the horrible day in January when her granduncle's house in Jerusalem was bombed by a group of mysterious girls in black robes. Were *they* servants of the Demon? They had known about the scroll. And they had said that it would make a "fitting burnt offering" for somebody named Lilith. . . .

Wait a second.

How could the scroll make a burnt offering? It couldn't even *burn*. Were the Demon's servants unaware of the scroll's real powers? No, no—she was getting ahead of herself. She didn't even know if those girls were connected with the Demon. She shouldn't speculate. She had to finish deciphering the scroll first. She had to break the code Uncle Elijah had told her about. Until she did, she wouldn't know for sure what she was dealing with.

"What is it?" Ibrahim asked.

"I'm not sure," she muttered. She continued reading to herself again—past the part about the Seers' denying the Chosen One to her face . . . and then her gaze came to rest on the last few lines.

Oh, my God.

Her eyes widened. She gasped.

"Sarah? Is something wrong?"

She shook her head, unable to tear her gaze from the parchment. "It . . . it says that there's a traitor in our midst," she told him in a hollow voice. "It says that I'm going to lead my companions to death and ruin."

"That's impossible," Ibrahim proclaimed.

But dread settled over her—instantly and completely, like a black shroud. The scroll had *never* been wrong. Not once. "Do you think we're making a mistake? Maybe we shouldn't go to New York." Her voice rose. "Maybe we—"

"Sarah, *relax,*" he soothed. "Look at me."

She glanced up at him, shaking. How could he be so calm, so sure of himself? Didn't he understand what this meant? They were doomed—

"If there's a traitor in our midst, we'll find him," Ibrahim stated confidently. "Believe me. You're leading your companions to *life,* Sarah. Not death. You're taking them to a place where the melting plague doesn't exist."

She stared back at the prophecy. Ibrahim had a

point about where they were going; she'd proved it herself only minutes ago. But the words were right there in the scroll. The truth was right there.

He took her chin in his hand, gently turning her face toward his. "Listen to me. Things are different now. Before, you could only see the prophecies in hindsight. But now you're prepared. Now you can *avoid* something bad before it happens—"

"That's exactly what I'm talking about," Sarah interrupted. Her voice trembled. "If we can avoid this, maybe we should change course. Maybe we should go to a different city first, like Washington or Boston. Or maybe we should just stop in the water until we find the traitor."

Ibrahim shook his head. "New York is your home. I know how much it means to you to get back. We can turn around at the first sign of any trouble. We won't arrive for more than two weeks. That's plenty of time to find the traitor." His hand fell away from her, and his expression became grave. "I'll make it my mission to find him, Sarah. I promise."

Sarah stared back at him in silence.

Then she exhaled. Her muscles relaxed.

I know you will.

And incredibly enough, she believed it—all of it, everything he'd told her. He made her feel safe again. Just being in his presence, basking in the beauty of those intense black eyes . . . the sudden tension eased as fast as it had overcome her.

"Why are you so good to me?" she found herself asking.

He smiled. "Because I love you," he answered.

Sarah blinked. She'd heard him say those words more times than she could possibly count. Only weeks ago they would have sickened her—maybe even terrified her. But now they filled her with a warm reassurance, a comfort that she hadn't ever known . . . not even before the plague. She reached out and caressed his cheek. Hearing those words made her feel *whole*.

"You know something, Ibrahim?" she whispered. "I love you, too."

EIGHT

WIT Campus,
Babylon, Washington
May 15–19

May 15

So what is this notepad all about?
Is it supposed to keep me from going
insane or something? You didn't even
tell me what I'm supposed to do
with it. You just shoved it under
the door with a pencil. Maybe you
want me to write down all my
thoughts so you can find out some
juicy little secret before you kill me.
Fine. I can play that game. Do you
want to see my thoughts, Trevor?
Here they are. In no particular order:

1. How do you live with yourself
after what you did? Do you sleep at
night?

2. I won't waste paper explaining how much I hate you because it would take up a lot more space than this little pad.

3. I hereby disown you. You're not my brother anymore. I always used to joke around that you'd turn into a serial killer—one of those guys who chops people up and uses the body parts to fertilize his flower garden. The truth is way more sick.

4. I pray that Brian is still alive so he can make good on his promise to come back and burn this place down.

5. See numbers 1 through 4.

May 16

Sorry, Trevor. My mood isn't as good as it was yesterday.

Three days have gone by since the

whole thing happened, and for the first time, it's actually hitting me. If you spend eighty straight hours locked in a classroom by yourself, you have a lot of time to think about stuff. You get very deep into your own thoughts. See, I know all about being alone. You probably know a lot about it, too. Before New Year's Eve you had no friends. You were always alone.

Now you're the most popular guy in town. Big man on campus, as they say.

Anyway, I hope you just get rid of me quickly because I don't think I can live with what I did. I'm serious. The way I see it, I killed about fifteen kids. Maybe more. I don't remember much except the shots and then a lot of blood and screaming, but I know a few of them managed to run off. I pray that they did.

True, you shot them down, but it's my fault. I brought them here. I basically promised them that I could make up with you and that you'd take care of them.

How do you like that?

It's strange. I keep thinking a lot about that intro to psych course. It really helped me figure people out. Including myself. I think I passed through the four stages of grief. Now I'm ready to pay the price for what I did. So take your best shot at me, Trevor. I'm all set.

May 17

Where do you get off? You grab me and leave me rotting in here for four days, totally cut off from everything and everyone, then you have the nerve to ask me for advice about Jezebel? Well. Being as I kept my mouth shut when you were in here, I'll say it now: Go to hell.

And let me tell you something else. That chick was always a psycho. That's why I dug her so much. She'll do anything. So in answer to your question: Yes. You better watch out. She can tell what people are thinking. I could never hide anything from her. She probably does have psychic powers. Man, oh, man. It almost makes me laugh. I never thought I'd hear you spout off about supernatural mumbo jumbo. You really flipped, didn't you?

Anyway, it's nice to know that she managed to break out of here, at least for a little while. She must have really freaked you out. Too bad she only made it as far as the TV room. How did she do it?

P.S. I hope you die.

I guess the Jezebel thing really pissed you off, huh? Is that why you stopped feeding me? That's pretty classy, Trevor. Killing your own flesh and blood by starvation. You never cease to outdo yourself. So I guess the only reason you didn't shoot me in the first place was because you thought I could tell you something about your new girlfriend. How sweet.

You know what? I used to think that being alone was the worst thing in the world. I used to think that if I ever got stuck in solitary

confinement, like I am now, I'd
probably die.

Now I know that some things are a
whole lot worse.

Knowing that you killed a lot
of people is one of them. So is
knowing that you outlived your
usefulness. So is hunger. Real
hunger, not just an empty stomach.
The kind of hunger that makes you
think about eating chipped paint
off the walls because you think it
might dull the pain.

I really hope you read this so
you can see how successful you are.

Congratulations, Trevor. You did
it. You broke me.

May 19

I'm going to have to ask you a
favor. Okay? You win. I give you
that. You win. You're smarter than me,
and better than me, and you're in

charge. You finally got what you wanted. If I could tell you anything important about Jezebel, I would. I honestly told you everything that I know already.

But I'm going to die in this classroom, Trevor. Just the way you planned. So I need you to do something for me. Just look inside yourself, and try to remember that there's a human being in there somewhere who can feel love and happiness and all the rest of that stuff that you and I never talk about. I know there is. I still know you as well as anyone else.

Anyway, I'm going to make a confession.

It has to do with a boy who came here with me. His name is Caleb Walker. He's skinny and tall, and he has long hair. I don't know if he managed to run away before you shot him. But if he's alive and you know where he is, I want you to tell him something for me. Please.

Tell him that I wasn't honest with him or myself. Tell him that I always had feelings for him but that I never admitted it because I was scared of getting hurt. Tell him that if I could go back in time, I would have done things a lot differently. Tell him that I love him.

It sounds crazy, I know. But you have to do it.

Thank you, Trevor. I mean it. If anyone can pull this off, you can. And I'll owe you. You and I will be brother and sister again. I don't know if that means anything to you, but it does to me.

I know you'll see it in your heart to make me happy.

NINE

Outside the WIT Campus,
Babylon, Washington
Night of May 20

Caleb was beginning to get worried. He knew that if he kept hanging around in front of this college or whatever the hell it was, he'd probably get shot.

That wasn't what worried him, though. What worried him was that he didn't *care*.

He was a perfect target. He stood right next to the barbed wire fence, not ten feet from a huge bonfire on the other side. The entire driveway was bathed in a bright orange-white light. There were no locusts to offer any cover, either. The fire must have driven them out. He might as well have been standing in the middle of a stage, wearing a sign that said: Kill Me!

But he felt nothing.

Well, almost nothing. The only thing he felt was a vague and mildly unsettling emptiness. He'd felt the same way when Ariel bolted from the hotel the morning after he met Leslie. But there was no comparison between *that* and what he'd experienced in the past week. None. Seven nights ago he saw a dozen kids murdered. This morning a girl died in his arms from gunshot wounds. But he hadn't been sad, or scared, or angry, or *anything*. Every emotion

81

seemed to pass straight through his body like water through a sieve.

I must be going crazy.

Maybe it was time to start drinking again. Yeah. That would help. *Definitely.* Too many weeks had passed since he'd gotten bombed. It was really a shame that Leslie didn't party. As cool as she was, she was kind of overly obsessed with her health. On the other hand, her conservative lifestyle did do wonders for her appearance. No doubt. She was *fine.* But in a weird way, she was almost too good-looking. She didn't have the same burnt-out charm that Ariel did—

Is somebody sneaking up on me?

There was a shuffling noise behind him. It was barely audible over the crackling flames—but he could hear the soft, uneven crunching of dead locusts . . . slowly approaching, drawing closer and closer. He didn't even bother to turn around. What was the point? It was probably Ariel's brother. Maybe he was going to put a knife in Caleb's back. But Caleb was too tired to fight. He was too tired to even *run.*

"Caleb!"

He jumped. *Leslie?* He spun around. Why was she tiptoeing around out here?

"I've been looking all over for you!" she whispered. She looked frazzled. Her eyebrows were knit. For once her long black hair was a mess. She hid behind him, crouching slightly, casting a furtive glance toward the nearest building. "What are you doing here? It isn't safe."

Caleb shrugged. "I know. What are you—"

"So what's the deal?" she whispered. She grabbed

his arm. "We have to get out of here! Somebody could see us!"

"In a minute," he mumbled. He stared up over the tips of the flames at a row of darkened windows. "I want to see if I can spot Ariel. I know she's in there."

Leslie shook her head, tugging at him. "She's probably dead by now, Caleb," she muttered. "I don't mean to be harsh, but you're not using your head. This is *dumb.*"

"Maybe it is," he answered calmly. "But if there's any chance she's still alive, I want to find out about it."

"And then what?" she snapped. She glanced at the building again, and her voice fell back to a whisper. "Why are you so worried about her, anyway? This whole thing is Ariel's fault. For all you know, she *knew* what was going to happen. Maybe she's in there living it up right now. Maybe she was in on it from the start."

No! Caleb batted her hand from his arm. Anger swept over him. But it was like a cleansing rain, a thunderstorm that cleared the stagnant air in his head. Finally. He was *feeling* something again—something potent and real.

"Don't say that," he snarled. "You don't know Ariel."

"Do *you?*" she cried, glaring at him in the firelight. "Think about it, Caleb. You've only known her for a few months. And you were wasted that whole time, so you couldn't—"

"Can I help you two?"

Oh, jeez.

A squat, tubby, pale-faced kid stepped out from

behind the bonfire and strode over to the fence. He was carrying a double-barreled shotgun, which he promptly cocked and lowered at Caleb and Leslie.

Caleb stiffened.

"Hey, hey—we're sorry," Leslie breathed. She held up her hands. "Please. We don't want any trouble. Just let us get out of here, and you'll never see us again. I swear—"

"Come here," the boy ordered.

Oh, no. Caleb stepped forward, but the boy jerked his gun at him.

"Just the girl," he growled. "I want to see her in the light."

Caleb held his breath. He shot a quick glance at Leslie. She stared back at him. Her body was shaking. But she took three steps toward the gate.

"Closer," the boy commanded.

Leslie shuffled forward another few inches. Her tan skin glowed a golden brown in the light of the roaring flames.

"Hello, there." A smile spread across the boy's face. "What's your name?"

She shook her head. "Please, just—"

"Your *name!*" he barked.

"Leslie," she whispered. "It's Leslie."

The boy nodded. "Hi, Leslie. It's a pleasure to meet you. My name's Barney. And today's your lucky day. You're coming with me—"

"Let her go," Caleb interrupted.

The boy raised his gun and pointed it directly at Caleb's face.

Caleb took a step back. A rapid and uneven rhythm filled his ears. Several seconds passed before he realized it was his own heart.

"This has nothing to do with you," the boy stated. He jerked his head at Leslie. "There's a hole in the fence about twenty feet to your right. But I'm sure both of you know about that." He smiled again, then turned back toward Caleb. "Leslie, would you be so kind as to step through the hole and join me?"

Leslie didn't move. "Please," she croaked. "I promise we—"

"Do it now," the boy insisted. "Or your friend here dies."

I'm probably gonna die, anyway, Caleb thought. *Make a run for it, Leslie. Just bolt—*

But Leslie ducked around the fence and through the hole, then hurried over to the boy.

Caleb shook his head. It was unbelievable. He'd lost *her* now, too. He'd lost everything. His stomach turned. This whole mess was his fault. Leslie wouldn't even be here if she hadn't come to find him.

The boy shifted the gun to his right hand and wrapped his left around Leslie's waist. "Beat it, jackass," he ordered. "Today's your lucky day, too. I'm not going to kill you. There's been too much killing already."

"Wait!" Caleb called.

The boy scowled.

"I just . . . look." He stared at Leslie imploringly. "Just do me a favor, okay? When you see Ariel, tell her . . ." He couldn't bring himself to finish. "Tell her . . ."

And then Leslie smiled.

She nodded to him—just barely—as if she were

saying: *You don't need to utter another word. I understand. It's okay.*

"I'll tell her," she whispered.

The boy lowered his gun and shoved her roughly toward the building.

Without waiting to see what happened next, Caleb sprinted down the driveway and back into the locust-filled night.

**Amarillo,
Texas
Night of May 21**

Today I looked back through my old diary entries. Reading them was like reading the words of a stranger. I found one from last month where I wrote about having a secret. The secret was that I didn't know who I was anymore. And when I read it, I burst into tears because that isn't really a secret at all—it's just a feeling, a fleeting sort of emotion, and everything was really okay. I was just confused. And it makes me so sad because I never appreciated how happy I was even when I was going through a rough time. I had so much going for me.

Now I know what a real secret is.

I know because I'm pregnant.

I can't deny it anymore. I've missed my period twice in a row now. At first I thought it was because I wasn't getting enough vitamins, or that my body was out of sorts from all the stress and traveling, or that I'd caught some kind of virus. I didn't even want to write about it in here. It was too scary. I guess I was praying.

But nine weeks have passed since George and I made love for the first time, and the symptoms are all there. I'm tired all the time. I throw up in the morning. I even think about hamburgers constantly—how nice it would be to eat one. It's exactly how my biology teacher said it would be in sex education.

I really wish I skipped school that day. Then I wouldn't be so certain.

I can't stop crying. What am I going to do? George has no idea. I keep avoiding him, and he thinks it's because we're still in a fight about the Healer—which is true, I guess. I can't understand why he doesn't see the truth. He spends all day out in the fields, looking and looking for something, torturing himself trying to prove that the Healer is a fake, that the Chosen One is someone else, a girl. It's taken over his life.

I have so many fears. Can the Healer help us? Will our baby even survive when it's born? The melting plague killed all the children on New Year's Eve, right along with the adults. I have to tell George, but I can't bring myself to speak to him. I still love him so much. The worst part of all is that he doesn't realize how much he's hurting me. He thinks he's doing the right thing.

Julia drew in a quivering breath. It was time to stop. If she wrote any more, she'd start bawling again. Besides, it was getting dark, and a meeting was about to start in the barn. The sun had already sunk below the horizon. In the twilight the dead cornfields seemed void of color, almost bluish gray. It was so depressing.

But she donned a mask of false happiness. She *had* to; she had to maintain the illusion that everything was fine. Nobody could know the truth. With a sigh she closed the small, weather-beaten notebook and shoved it into the pocket of her white gown. Then she pushed herself out of the dust and strolled to the open barn door. The buzz of conversation was already leaking into the night.

"Hi, Julia!" Linda sang out. "I saved a seat for you."

"Thanks." Julia forced a smile. *I should just turn around and leave.*

No. That would mean that something was wrong. Besides, the sight of this cozy, candlelit barn *was* comforting, in a way. Wasn't it? She loved these meetings—these informal weekly sessions where all the Seers sat in a circle and talked freely about their visions. In a very real way, these kids were family. They were all brothers and sisters, bound by a common thread. And the number was growing—new Seers arrived at the Promised Land every day. They all found comfort in one another.

Except for George, of course. He refused to participate.

But there was no point in thinking about *that*— unless she wanted to cry for the hundredth time. She plodded across the straw-covered floor and slumped down in a folding chair beside Linda. "How's it going?" she asked as cheerfully as she could.

"Not bad," Linda replied. "Aren't you feeling well? You look tired."

Julia shrugged. "I'm fine," she said. But the words stuck in her throat.

"Are you sure?" Linda asked.

Julia nodded vigorously. *Smile!* she commanded herself. *Don't give it away!* She blinked several times.

"It's George, isn't it?"

"I—I think I'm just worn out," Julia stammered. *Please leave me alone.* She couldn't talk about George—not here, not now. She'd lose it. She was already teetering on the brink of another breakdown.

"You know, Julia, if you ever want to discuss anything with me, you can," Linda murmured. "I mean it. If there's—"

"Welcome, everyone," a voice burst from the loudspeaker.

A trembling sigh escaped Julia's lips. *Thank the Lord.* The Healer had arrived. More importantly, he had shut Linda up. Julia didn't mean to be rude or harsh; she just needed to sort things out on her own. Later. But this meeting would help her forget things, wouldn't it? As long as she could lose herself in a discussion, she could keep playing the charade.

"So." The Healer's resonant voice boomed across the barn. "Who would like to start?"

"I would," a boy answered right away.

Julia turned to him. *All right. Time to concentrate. Time to clear my mind.* What was this guy's name again? He was familiar: frail looking with sleepy brown eyes . . . Gene. Yes. He was at the very first meeting. Back then Gene thought that the

Chosen One was female—just the way Julia once had. But over the past few weeks he'd also come to see the truth. Maybe he could talk some sense into George. It was worth a try. *Anything* was.

Gene cleared his throat and glanced awkwardly around the circle. "Something's been bothering me lately." He paused, then looked up at the loudspeaker. "Ever since the locusts died, um . . . I've sort of felt the pull again."

"The pull?" the Healer demanded.

"Yeah." Gene's eyes darted around the circle again. "The pull out west. I'm sure everybody here knows what I mean."

Julia nodded. *Yes.* This was important. She felt the pull again, too—only she was far too preoccupied to pay much attention to it. Whenever she thought about that strange urge to travel west, she always imagined a giant horseshoe magnet, a hundred stories tall, perched on the Pacific Coast and dragging her across the country. But the pull didn't make any sense, at least not *now.* Why were they still feeling it if they had already reached the Promised Land?

"I've been feeling it, too," somebody else muttered.

"Yeah," Linda agreed. "Me too."

"What do you think it means?" the Healer asked.

Gene shook his head. "I thought maybe it was because we're running out of food here," he said hesitantly. "Maybe we're supposed to pick up and move. But . . ." He bit his lip.

"Go on," the Healer encouraged.

"Maybe it's the *Demon* who wants us to go west," Gene suggested. "Have you ever thought of that? I mean, I still have the same vision. The Demon sneaks up behind me and puts a blindfold over my eyes. And it happens right as I'm about to tell the Chosen One . . ." He swallowed. "I'm about to tell you that there's a traitor nearby."

"*I* see the traitor, too!" a girl on the other side of the circle cried.

Everyone turned at once.

The girl flushed. "Well, I don't *see* him, or her, or whoever it is," she admitted. "I'm in a boat, lost in a heavy fog. The Chosen One—*you*, I mean . . . you're in a boat near me. And I'm calling to you to watch out because the traitor is in the water, too."

The traitor? Julia turned the word over in her mind. She'd never heard anyone mention a traitor before. What did that have to do with the pull, or the Demon, or going west?

The barn fell silent.

Julia fiddled with one of her curls. This meeting wasn't making her feel any better at all. No. Every new revelation added to the confusion. She felt as if *she* were the one lost in a fog. All of the visions were crazy. Particularly hers. She still saw the same thing, over and over again—the same gruesome image of her plunging a sword into the Demon's belly.

"I think Gene is right," Linda suddenly announced. "I think the Demon *is* pulling us out west. And I think she wants us to go *now*—before we're ready."

There was a squeak in the loudspeaker, as if the Healer were adjusting something. "Explain that to me."

Linda settled back in her chair. "I've been thinking a lot about this. I may be wrong, but I think every one of our visions is like a single ingredient in a recipe. Alone, they don't make much sense. But taken all together, as one, they form something complete. I think it's the recipe of how we're going to help you defeat the Demon."

Hold on a minute. . . .

Julia shook her head. Was that possible?

"So they're all parts of a bigger picture?" somebody asked excitedly.

Linda nodded.

Julia could feel excitement, too. It was contagious. They were on to something here, something *big*. Linda's words made sense. They made perfect sense, as a matter of fact. She had to be right. No wonder Julia hadn't heard of the traitor. That wasn't her "ingredient."

"So we have to take all the visions and fit them together, right?" somebody asked. "It's like a puzzle. We have to find all the Seers. Because if there's one ingredient missing . . ."

"The recipe won't be complete," Linda finished.

Incredible. Of course! Julia felt as if her brain had suddenly been plugged in again. And for a few mercurial and delirious moments, she was actually *happy*. Now it seemed as if they had a chance. Manic scenes flashed through her head: She saw herself giving birth; she saw George weeping with joy over their baby; she saw the three of them marching out west with the Healer and an army of Seers to destroy the Demon forever. . . .

But then the gloom and uncertainty returned.

What am I so happy about? I still haven't told George the truth.

And that wasn't the only problem. There was no way *all* the Seers would make it to the Promised Land. What if some of them vaporized? What if some of them ended up in the hands of those girls from Ohio—the ones who had nearly killed her and George? Hidden dangers lurked everywhere. If every single vision *were* an essential ingredient, then the "recipe" was probably already ruined.

"So we'll eventually go west," Gene stated in the silence. "We'll eventually battle the Demon, after we figure it all out."

"Right," Linda replied. "But we have to resist the temptation to leave too early. We have to wait until all the Seers get in the Promised Land."

"But there's no way they're all going to make it!" Julia cried.

Linda raised her eyebrows. "I didn't say it was going to be *easy*," she muttered wryly. "I just said we'll have to wait."

Julia frowned. Did Linda think this was *funny?*

But all at once she realized something.

Linda wasn't trying to make a joke out of it. She was just saying that there was no point in worrying about circumstances beyond their control. And that was the perfect attitude. Because if they couldn't keep a sense of humor, if they couldn't remain optimistic . . . then the battle was already lost.

George was right—Linda *was* sharp. She was more than that. She was wise. Why couldn't Julia be more like her? Why did she always get herself into trouble? Why did she always just accept the worst—and never try to find her way out of a bad situation?

"Then it's decided," the Healer announced. "We'll remain here until more Seers arrive. And in the meantime we'll focus our efforts on finding the traitor. We'll make it our first priority—after gathering supplies and planting new crops."

But Julia was hardly paying attention. No. She was thinking: *I have to take charge of my life. For once I'm going to do something smart. I'm going to be more like Linda. I'm going to talk to George and tell him the truth. As soon as possible. He has just as much a right to know as I do. It's his baby, too. We're going to tackle this together.*

PART III;

May 22–31

The Fifth Lunar Cycle

Naamah was very, very pleased.

Her plans were proceeding more smoothly than anticipated. Overall, she'd experienced very few setbacks. The grand masquerade was unfolding one step at a time . . . and each step was more cunning and intricate than the next.

The extermination of the locusts was a work of art on par with the destruction of the Aswan High Dam. Naamah had expected a little more trouble. The gullibility of the Seers was almost shocking. Virtually all of them accepted the absurd excuse that the lingering stench of DDT came from the dead insects. Almost all of them believed that their prayer and their faith in the Healer had produced the miracle.

All but one, in fact.

Yes, George Porter was proving to be quite a nuisance. Naamah hadn't counted on him to be so dogged in his efforts to expose the False Prophet. His visions were clearly more powerful than those of the others. But he was just one voice, a lone dissident, an outcast. And Naamah had already set a trap—a neat and tidy means of disposing of him, using the very tools she had used to subdue and deceive the flock. Soon he would be dead, and nobody would ever doubt the Healer or his miracles again . . . least of all Harold himself.

That was the most beautiful part of all.

Harold was convinced that he had played the key role in ridding the Promised Land of locusts. And he'd done nothing. He'd simply imbibed the drugged water and slept the same rich, stuporous sleep of his flock—while the hooded Lilum were busy at work, spraying his fields.

He was also convinced that he had won his first battle against the Demon. And the Demon hadn't even brought the locusts upon him. No, Lilith had absolutely nothing to do with it. Such a plague was beyond even the range of her awesome powers—just as the other natural disasters were, the floods and earthquakes and rain.

A deeper magic was responsible, a magic as old as the earth itself.

But knowledge was Lilith's weapon. The hidden prophecies foretold of the catastrophes in the Final Year. It had been plainly written: Locusts invade the Americas on the second day of the fifth lunar cycle. And once again Lilith used the words as a means to her own ends.

Lilith understood her limits. She was an immortal; she was privy to the secrets of the Code and Prophecies; she could possess a human being—but she was not omnipotent.

Yet at the same time, certain elements of the future were not set in stone. So Lilith exploited the wondrous technology of humanity to defeat humanity. Naamah couldn't help but laugh. There was a delicious irony in that, wasn't there? DDT, Nembutal, radio beacons that broadcast recycled commercials on continuous loops . . . and, of course, the Russian weapons that caused the melting plague: These were Lilith's implements of destruction.

The human race was like clay in Lilith's hands. She molded them with both truth and lies—for truth, like knowledge, could also be deadly.

It was true, for instance, that every vision was a

piece in a grand puzzle. Naamah took it upon herself to plant that very idea in the minds of the Seers. They would have figured it out for themselves sooner or later, of course. But now they trusted her.

Now they believed her when she insisted that they had to fight the temptation to go west.

Now they believed her when she stated that they had to gather in the same place.

And now Lilith was poised to wipe them out in one master stroke.

But time was short. Month by month, the countdown continued, drawing inexorably toward the final moment when the fate of the world would teeter on a single act.

So Naamah was on a tight schedule.

Every piece had yet to fall into place. . . .

CHAPTER
ELEVEN

Ten days came and went before George found something that even *might* have been suspicious. He spotted it around nine in the morning, out at the eastern edge of Harold's property. It was a hole filled with dozens of little plastic prescription pill bottles. They were half buried in the dirt. Most of the labels had been scraped off. And it was clear that they'd been scraped off in a hurry, too—because he could still read a few of them.

They all said the same thing: Nembutal.

Too bad he had no clue what that was.

"What's Nembutal?" George asked Harold later in the day.

Harold smirked. "Why? Are you having trouble sleeping?"

"Just answer the question," George said.

"It's a depressant," he replied. "A barbiturate, to be more exact."

A barbiturate. George's eyes narrowed. Those were drugs that made people pass out, right? "Does it have any side effects?" he asked.

102

"It can." Harold shrugged. "Dry mouth, headache, nausea . . ."

George nodded. "Like a hangover?"

"I suppose." Harold smiled. "What's this about, George?"

George just shook his head. It suddenly occurred to him that he was acting just like a cop. Wow. He never thought *that* would happen. But he'd combed every square inch of this farm, and he still didn't know if his discovery proved a damn thing—other than that Harold had once had a stash of barbiturates. Only cops would waste their time doing something like that.

"Well?" Harold asked. "Why the sudden curiosity in barbiturates?"

"I'll let you know, Harold," George said. "I'll let you know."

That afternoon George returned to the hole. He crouched beside it and studied it for a very long time. The dirt in the immediate area had been dug up unevenly. As far as George could tell, somebody had done a really bad job of trying to bury the bottles—which probably meant that they had been pressed for time.

So the question was this: Why would somebody rush to hide this kind of trash?

George could think of only one reason. Harold must have spiked the water supply with Nembutal on the night everybody supposedly "prayed." Then, once the flock was out cold, he sprayed the fields with some kind of insecticide. Being as there were so many acres, the job probably took all night—which meant he didn't have a lot of time to get rid of the evidence that he'd duped everyone.

Pretty freaking smart, huh?

Not quite.

Still . . . George *knew* he needed something more if he was going to prove his theory. He couldn't be too eager. He'd spent enough time in juvenile court to know that circumstantial evidence like this could be explained away in seconds—especially by a smooth talker like Harold.

But it was enough to get started. It was the first step. And at the very least, it was enough to convince someone else that Harold might be trying to cover something up.

So George grabbed a bottle from the pile, shoved it in his pocket, then hurried back to the barn.

"George, where are you taking me?" Julia demanded. Her voice sounded scratchy. She yawned once, stumbling behind him in the darkness. "I can't see a thing. It must be three in the morning—"

"Just a little farther," George promised. "Over that hill." He took her hand and led her gently across the barren landscape. Although he had brought a candle, he didn't want to light it until they reached the hole. He didn't want to risk being spotted, not even all the way out here. Besides, his eyes had adjusted plenty to the moonlight.

"What's this all about, anyway?" She was sounding grumpier and grumpier. "Why won't you tell me?"

"I want you to see for yourself, okay?" George replied.

All of a sudden she stopped dead in her tracks.

Her fingers slipped from George's grasp.

"What's wrong?" George asked. He was losing patience. He turned to face her. "We're almost there."

"I , uh . . ." She chewed her lip and stared down at her feet. Her long curls fell in front of her face, hiding her expression from him. "George, there's something I have to tell you," she mumbled. "It's—well, it's . . . important. It's a big deal."

Uh-oh. Something in her voice sent a twinge of alarm through him. Her tone was all stiff and formal—as if she were distancing herself from him, as if she were talking to a stranger. His mind raced. She didn't want to break up, did she?

"It has to do with us," she murmured. She kicked at the dirt.

"Yeah?" he croaked. His pulse picked up a few beats. An uncomfortable heat spread across his face and chest. "What about us?"

She sniffed once. Her body seemed to be trembling.

George leaned forward and eyed her closely. *Oh, no . . .*

She was *crying*.

"What is it?" he whispered. He reached for her hand but stopped himself. Touching her might be a bad idea; he didn't know what to do. "What's wrong?"

Julia didn't answer. Tears trickled down her cheeks.

This was bad. He needed to do something. *Fast.*

"Okay—okay, listen," he stammered desperately. "I was gonna wait to show you the whole pile of bottles . . . but I, uh, I got one in my pocket. Look. I found proof that Harold is a fake. I mean, it's not total proof, but it—"

"No!" she wailed. She stamped her foot and shook her head, sobbing uncontrollably now. "Don't *talk* about that! That's not what this is about!"

George swallowed. He'd never seen her like this before; she'd never been so distraught. "Shhh," he whispered. He was shaking now, too. "Just take it easy, okay? Lemme just show you—"

A blinding white glare silenced him.

What the—

His stomach plummeted. He stepped away from Julia and shielded his eyes, swept up in a wholly familiar panic. He felt exactly like he had on New Year's Eve, when those cops hit him with a searchlight.

"So here he is," an all-too-familiar voice proclaimed. "The traitor."

Harold. George made a face. He should have known he'd never get away with proving anything. He should have kept his mouth shut. Asking about the Nembutal was stupid. This whole thing was a crock from the start. Obviously Harold never expected George to actually *find* something. So now the jerk was covering his tracks.

"What do you have to say for yourself?" Harold demanded.

"Bite me," George spat back automatically.

Harold snickered. The light shifted to Julia. She

106

blinked a few times, squinting. Her moist cheeks glistened. George lowered his hands and peered into the darkness at Harold. He was about ten feet away, holding a powerful military-type flashlight . . . but he wasn't alone. Two dopey-looking meatheads were standing right beside him.

And so was Linda.

George gasped. What the hell was *she* doing out here?

"Come here, Julia," Harold commanded.

"No!" George barked. He stepped forward—but the light flew back in his face, stinging his pupils. He flinched and turned away from it.

"Easy, George," Harold scolded playfully. "You don't have to worry about Julia. She's going to be just fine. If I were you, I'd worry more about yourself." He paused. "Search him."

The next thing George knew, he was being seized in a painful stranglehold.

"Hey!" he protested, wincing.

But he couldn't move. Somebody snapped his neck forward and twisted his arms behind his back. The light still shone in his face. His eyes were smarting. A pair of hands slapped his jeans' pockets. Fingers squeezed the empty pill bottle through the denim. With a jerky movement the fingers yanked the bottle free, leaving the pocket turned inside out.

"Here it is," a thick voice announced.

The flashlight shifted for a moment, up to the bottle. One of the meatheads held it over his head as if he'd just won a prize—a pathetic little glowing amber trophy.

"Well, well," Harold mused. "It looks like you've already removed the pills. Either that or you've taken them all. In which case you don't have much longer to live."

George gave a short laugh. *"I* took the pills? Nice try, ass—" The stranglehold tightened. He grunted in pain. "You know that's bull, Harold," he choked out.

"Is it?" Harold asked dryly. He turned the light back in George's eyes.

"You used the pills," George growled. He tried to squirm free, but it was useless. "Julia, listen to me. This is what I was gonna tell you about. Harold drugged us that night. He tried to cover it up. But I found the empty bottles out here. He tried to bury them."

Harold laughed again. "That's *very* creative, George. Now let me tell Julia what really happened. Linda had insomnia this evening. She came to me and asked for a pill to help her sleep. When I searched for my supply of Nembutal, I found that it was missing. But I had a hunch as to where it might have gone, being as George asked me about it today." He sighed. "In a way, it was a blessing that Linda couldn't sleep. She was the one who saw you sneak out of the barn and head off in this direction. It's quite ironic, isn't it?"

Rage burned inside George's twisted body. "That's not true!" he shrieked.

Harold sniffed disdainfully. "Which part? Tell me something, George—did you ask me about the drugs *before* you stole them? Or did you steal them first and ask me later?"

"This is crap." George tried to shake his head. "I *found* the empty bottles, Harold. You know it. I found all of them. I can show you right now!"

There was a pause. "You found them," Harold said. "I see. Now which is more likely? That I single-handedly drugged my entire flock, yet carelessly left the bottles strewn about my property . . . or that you, a known criminal and substance abuser, deliberately violated the commandments of the Promised Land?" His voice hardened. "Who would you believe, given the circumstances?"

Oh, God. This was a setup, wasn't it? George could feel the panic welling up inside him once again. This whole thing stunk. Yup. He knew when he'd been suckered. Harold wanted him to find these bottles. Harold wanted to have somebody on whom he could place the blame—a patsy, an out.

"You planned it this way," George whispered. "You wanted to pin the missing pills on me from the start. . . ."

Harold snorted. "How clever of me."

"It's true! You know it!"

"Let's ask your girlfriend." The light flashed to Julia. "Who does *she* believe? Does she believe the Chosen One? Or does she believe the traitor?"

George shifted his gaze away from the light, looking at Julia. Just seeing the wounded expression on her face hit him like a punch to the stomach.

Julia blinked at George.

Then she buried her face in her hands and wept.

"Well," Harold murmured. "I think her silence speaks for itself, don't you?"

George gaped unbelievingly at Julia from under the painful headlock. *You can't let this happen!* Didn't she feel anything for him anymore? He loved her! What was her problem? "Please, Julia," he begged. "Please . . ."

But before he could say anything more, Harold nodded to one of the boys.

A white flash exploded in George's brain, and he slipped instantly into unconsciousness.

TWELVE

WIT Campus,
Babylon, Washington
Night of May 25

"Jeez, Ariel, you really changed a lot," Trevor remarked, flipping through the pages of the yellow legal pad. "You got so sensitive. I mean, listen to what you wrote. 'I know you'll see it in your heart to make me happy.'" He snorted. "That doesn't sound like you at all. It's so dorky. It's so unhip."

Screw you, Ariel silently shot back. She wouldn't even look up at him. She had to hold on to some shred of dignity. And it was a pretty hard thing to do, being as she sat hunched on the dirty classroom floor, feverishly shoveling undercooked spaghetti into her mouth with her bare hands. From a filthy metal bowl, no less. Trevor took extra care *not* to give her any other utensils so he could see her make a pig out of herself. It was a nice touch, wasn't it? Yeah. It showed real style.

"You know, maybe you got that line from one of those teen romance novels you used to read," he said. "This smells like plagiarism to me."

Ha, ha, ha. What a comedian. It was amazing: He still spoke in the same creeped-out, robotic-sounding monotone. Maybe he *was* a robot. Maybe her real

111

brother had been switched at birth with some weird, futuristic, cybernetic organism—like in *The Terminator*. But no . . . then Trevor wouldn't look so much like her. So maybe her brother's insides had just been replaced with computer parts, like a *Bionic Man* type of scenario. Yeah. Whatever the case, the . . . thing standing in front of her definitely wasn't human. No way.

Trevor chuckled. "And what about this part up here? It says—"

"Is there a point to this?" she interrupted. But her mouth was full, and the question sounded more like: "Mff-mm roint to diss?" Bits of noodle spewed onto her grubby jeans. She didn't bother to wipe them off. Nope. If Trevor wanted her to act like an animal, then she would indulge him. She would disgust *him* as much as she was disgusting herself. So she seized the bowl with both hands, threw back her head, and dumped the remainder of the spaghetti into her mouth. A few strands dangled across her chin—but she sucked them right up: *schlurp*.

Then she belched.

"Please, Ariel," Trevor chided. "You're being gross."

Ariel swallowed the rest of the doughy stuff down in one painful gulp. Then she took a deep breath. *"I'm* being gross?" she asked. She burped again. Finally she glanced up at him. "Lemme ask you something," she said, tossing the bowl aside with a noisy clatter. "Just, you know, a hypothetical sort of thing. Have you ever gone a week without food?"

Trevor sneered. He didn't answer. Instead he leaned against the wall and silently returned to reading the pitiful, desperate, humiliating words she'd written on that pad. *Man*. She shouldn't have given in.

"You should've paid more attention in school," he muttered. "Your grammar stinks—"

"How about two days?" she pressed. "Have you ever gone two days without food? It isn't making me *happy* to eat like this. I don't even *want* to eat. I don't want to give you the satisfaction. But I don't have any control. Hunger is an amazing thing, Trevor. It makes you realize that people aren't that much different from dogs or cats or rats—"

"That's enough philosophical BS for today, Ariel," he interrupted in a flat voice, without looking up. "Sheesh. I guess you haven't changed *that* much. You still love to hear yourself talk." He tossed the notebook back on the floor. He turned to leave, then paused and frowned at her. "By the way, what's up with that necklace? It's the ugliest thing I've ever seen."

Nice one, Trevor.

He always had to get in one last cheap shot, didn't he?

Her blood simmered. It wasn't even that she was offended. No, he was right: The necklace was ugly. She hadn't even thought about it in over a month. The stained silver pendant looked like an off-kilter ticktacktoe board. But in a weird sort of way, it represented everything that was so vile about him. After all, the necklace had been given to her by some Looney Tunes character who believed in the Chosen One. And Trevor got his jollies by *imprisoning* that kind of people. For a crazed instant Ariel had a vivid hallucination of ripping the pendant off the chain, jumping up, and stabbing Trevor through the eyeball with it. That would put it to good use.

"Oh, I almost forgot," Trevor added. He put his hand on the doorknob and turned his back to her. "The reason I came in here was to tell you that the rest of your friends are dead. We found them out by the mill. None of them got away this time."

Ariel gaped at him.

No, you didn't.

A sudden pain shot through her stomach, but she ignored it. She ignored the chill that rattled her weakened frame. It couldn't be true. Those kids would never have stayed around here—not after the shooting. Especially not Caleb. He was already freaked out *before* it happened. Trevor was just playing more of his sick mind games. That was why he was hiding his face; she could always tell when he was being dishonest.

"You're lying," she whispered.

Trevor shrugged and opened the door. "Whatever. But I can't tell what's-his-face that you loved him. It's a little too late for that. Sorry . . ."

You bastard! Ariel found herself leaping to her feet and lunging at him. But it was a lame attack; she felt as if she were watching somebody else—a loser, somebody beaten and pathetic. Trevor shoved her aside with a mere flick of his arm, sending her tumbling back to the floor. Her stomach heaved. The noodles seemed to be expanding inside her, threatening to surge back up her gullet.

"Don't touch me again, Ariel," Trevor warned. "Ever."

He stepped through the door and slammed it.

"Come back here!" she shrieked from the floor. "Come back. . . ." But her voice broke, and her words were lost in a fit of sobbing. Trevor's footsteps faded. What was her problem? She hated people who cried, who whined, who couldn't stand up for themselves. But she hated herself, didn't she? She hated herself for *everything:* for eating Trevor's food, for coming back here in the first place—for the horrible things she couldn't even think about. She curled up into a tight little ball. She just wanted to disappear. She wanted to sink through this floor and melt into the earth. . . .

The lock rattled.

It was turning. Ariel glanced up and wiped her face.

What now, Trevor? You want to show me pictures of Caleb's dead body?

The door swung open.

Ariel's eyes bulged.

It wasn't Trevor.

It was Leslie.

"What do you say we get out of this place?" Leslie asked with a smile.

This can't be happening, Ariel thought fearfully. *I must be seeing things. Trevor must have laced my spaghetti with—*

"Are you all right?" Leslie asked. Her smile faded. She leaned forward and extended a hand. "Come on. We probably don't have a lot of time."

Instinctively Ariel recoiled from her. There was no way Leslie could be here; Ariel must be having some kind of drug-induced apparition. Leslie looked so clean, so healthy—she even had new clothes. . . . *Wait a second.* Ariel recognized that black T-shirt. There was a Chinese dragon on it. She recognized those vinyl pants, too. Yeah. They belonged to *Jezebel*. How had Leslie gotten her hands on them? Or was Ariel's fried brain somehow producing a bizarre mix of the two girls? She couldn't deal with this. . . .

"Really, Ariel." Leslie glanced anxiously over her shoulder. "We gotta move."

Ariel shook her head. "What—what's going on?" she stammered. Her voice was no more than a whisper. "Are you real?"

"God, what have they done to you?" Leslie murmured. Her eyes softened; she bent down beside Ariel and gently wrapped her arms around Ariel's shoulders. "Of course I'm real. But you've gotta come with me now."

I can feel her hands on me, Ariel realized. She blinked a few times. *If she wasn't real, I wouldn't be able to feel her.*

Leslie hoisted Ariel to her feet and escorted her into the darkened corridor. Again Ariel felt as if she were standing outside herself and watching someone else. And she felt so drowsy, so spent—as if she'd just eaten a foot-long hoagie and washed it down with three or four beers. Could the noodles have done that to her? Maybe her stomach had shrunk or something. She was having a major food coma right now.

Either that or she really *was* on drugs.

"I think there's a door down here around the corner," Leslie muttered, glancing in either direction, then hurrying to the right. She shifted her arm to Ariel's waist and scooted her along. "This is the way I came in."

Ariel struggled to keep up as best she could. Her shuffling feet kept getting in the way of each other. "How'd you get in here?" she finally asked.

116

"Barney," Leslie whispered. She laughed grimly. "He gave me a special invitation. You know him? He's one of Trevor's soul mates."

Ariel's eyes narrowed. *Barney.* Nope. She had never paid any attention to Trevor's friends. He hardly had any friends.

"He's a fat little twerp who thinks he's God's gift to the human race," Leslie explained. "Anyway, he knows *you.* He said you were a burnout."

A burnout. Under normal circumstances, Ariel might have reacted to an insult like that. But her brain was just a little too disconnected right now.

Leslie jerked to a sudden stop in front of an open door. "You can take a look at him if you want. But make it snappy."

Ariel blinked. *Take a look at him?* She peered inside the dimly lit classroom. It smelled like rubbing alcohol. There was somebody on the floor: a pudgy little squirt with no shirt on, lying on his back with his tongue hanging out of his mouth. An empty mason jar lay overturned next to his head. The kid was *foul.* Little tufts of ratty hair covered his flabby chest. His fly was unzipped. She could see his underwear. He was wearing tighty whities. His belly burst out of them like a swollen balloon.

"He thinks *I'm* a burnout?" Ariel muttered.

Leslie chuckled. "Now there's the Ariel I know and love."

Ariel turned to her, grinning in spite of herself. "What did you do to him?"

Leslie smirked. "Boys are so predictable, don't you think? Especially horny, sexually deprived geeks."

117

She shook her head. "They'd sell their own mothers if they thought it would get them some play."

Ariel shook her head. "I, uh . . . don't quite get it."

"I told him that booze puts me in the mood," Leslie said with a shrug. "He and some of the other kids have been making their own moonshine behind Trevor's back. They use apples." Her smile widened. "Your brother doesn't really run as tight a ship as he thinks he does. Anyway, once Barney drank himself to la-la land, I swiped his master key."

Ariel glanced back at the beached whale on the floor. She was beginning to feel alert, alive—but her mind stewed with a million questions. What on earth was Leslie doing with this guy? How did she know so much about Trevor? Was she a prisoner here, too? She didn't look like a prisoner. . . .

"Look, Ariel, I want to apologize," Leslie murmured. "I said some things about you, and I thought . . . I blamed you for what happened. But now I know you were just trying to help us out. I *know* it. And I told Caleb that—"

"Caleb's still alive?" Ariel whispered, afraid of the answer.

Leslie nodded. "Yeah." She lowered her eyes. "But I said—"

"Don't worry about it," Ariel interrupted quickly. Suddenly everything seemed clear—she could think, she could move, and she could *feel*. "He's alive. That's all that matters. Let's bolt. You can explain everything to me later."

Leslie hesitated. She looked Ariel straight in the eye. "Caleb wanted me to tell you something," she said. "And . . . I'm—I'm sorry about the stuff that happened between him and me," she stammered. "I should have known better. Because he . . . he loves you."

He loves me?

Ariel froze. For a moment everything in the universe faded—everything but the image of Caleb's face in her mind. Ripples of delight spread through her entire body. So he felt the same way. The same way!

"I'm sorry," Leslie repeated.

"Sorry for what?" Ariel cried. "Leslie, you just made me happier than anybody's ever made me—" She broke off, remembering where she was. Her eyes shot back down the empty corridor. "I'm the one who should be sorry for acting like such a jerk to you," she whispered hastily. "You saved me twice now. So let's get out of here."

Leslie nodded.

A groan drifted out of the classroom. "Wassa?" Barney slurred. "Lessie, Less . . ."

The two of them dashed down the hall. Ariel kept her eyes peeled for any signs of trouble. But the entire building seemed almost deserted—except for a lone classroom light, fast approaching. Was Jezebel there? As they rounded the corner Ariel stole a quick peek through the window. She caught a glimpse of a profile, a blond head—

No!

Her legs instantly turned to liquid.

She couldn't run anymore. She clamped her hands over her mouth.

"Ariel, what is it?" Leslie hissed. Her eyes were wide. "Come on!"

"It's my ex-boyfriend," she whimpered. "It's Brian!"

She stared in terror at him—strapped to some kind of table, his eyes closed, his once healthy cheeks now drawn and sallow. He was naked except for a pair of boxer shorts—the same polka-dot boxers he'd worn on New Year's Eve. A lump filled her throat. He must be unconscious. . . .

Leslie pulled viciously at her arm. "We don't have time to get him. Barney's waking up. We have to go."

"But . . . but—"

"We'll get him later," Leslie stated. "We'll get everyone. I promise."

She didn't pause to argue anymore. She simply shoved Ariel down to the end of the hall, out the exit door, and into freedom.

THIRTEEN

**Cruise Ship *The Majestic*,
Approaching New York City
Early Morning, May 30**

Sarah was still half asleep by the time Ibrahim dragged her up onto the front deck. She blinked a few times and rubbed her eyes under her glasses. It must have been the middle of the night; she couldn't see a thing. The ship was moving very slowly—much more slowly than usual, in fact. It wasn't heaving as much, either. And it was so *quiet*. The distant purr of the engines was almost lost in the soft breeze.

"What's going on?" she asked groggily. She stifled a yawn.

Ibrahim draped his arm over her shoulders. "I wanted you to see for yourself," he whispered in her ear. He flung his other arm out into the inky darkness. "I wanted you to look upon it with your own eyes."

Sarah's eyes narrowed. She followed the direction of his outstretched finger . . .

And then she saw it.

Straight ahead, looming in a thick fog against the blue-black sky, was the unmistakable silhouette of a suspension bridge: two tall spires linked by a gently sloping upside-down arch.

"Oh, my God!" she cried. The sleepiness vanished,

121

replaced by an instant euphoria. She started laughing. "Ibrahim! We're here! We made it!"

He gave her a quick squeeze. "I know," he murmured. "I know."

"Where—where are we, exactly?" she stammered. She stood on her tiptoes and craned her neck, turning first one way and then the other. Two vast landmasses were drifting toward her on either side of the ship. The sky to her right was brightening a little, hinting vaguely at the first signs of morning. . . .

There! Sarah's heart jumped. She could just barely see the shadowy outlines of several tall, nondescript skyscrapers. But she couldn't get her bearings; all of it looked so unfamiliar. Where were the twin towers? Or the Empire State and Chrysler Buildings? If the sun was rising on her right, then they were heading north. Shouldn't they be heading east?

"I'm surprised at you, Sarah," Ibrahim teased. "I thought you'd recognize your hometown."

All at once it hit her. *Of course!*

"That's the Verrazano Bridge," she gasped.

"And right on the other side is the Statue of Liberty. I found a guidebook in the ship's library. I've never been to the States before, you know."

Sarah sighed and leaned against him. "Well, then. Let me be the first to welcome you to the USA."

I'm home. I'm really home.

For what seemed like a long time, she tried to enjoy the tranquility of the moment, the sight of the approaching bridge in the silence of the dawn—but she was simply too excited.

Before the sun set tonight, she would see her parents. She would sleep in her bedroom.

The thought of it left her breathless.

If only Josh could have made it, she thought, swallowing past the lump in her throat. *If only he could have seen what I'm seeing now. . . .*

"Where do you live?" Ibrahim asked. "Manhattan?"

"I never told you?" Sarah shook her head. It seemed funny that Ibrahim didn't know; he knew almost everything else about her. She shoved the memories of her dead brother from her mind. She'd mourn Josh later . . . with her parents. As a *family.* "Yeah. Seventy-eighth Street, between Madison and Park."

"In an apartment?"

Sarah managed a grin. "That's right. You'll see it for yourself today. Hey, I'll give you a sightseeing tour! How does that sound?"

"Fine," he answered. But he sounded distracted.

She glanced up at him. He was squinting at the Brooklyn skyline.

"I wonder why all the lights are out," he mumbled. He withdrew his arm from her shoulders and strolled over to the railing. "See what I mean? All the buildings are dark."

"Maybe they're trying to conserve energy," Sarah suggested. But she was thinking: *Who cares about lights? We're home!*

He shook his head. "What about the radio?" he asked gravely. "If they were trying to conserve energy, it seems odd that they would allow radio stations to keep operating at all hours."

"Ibrahim, listen to yourself!" Sarah cried. She

123

followed him to the railing and slipped her arm around his waist. "You sound totally paranoid. Maybe they let the radio stations operate in case there's any important news—they must know the rest of the world has been falling apart. Or maybe all the lights are out because everybody's *asleep*. Huh? Have you ever thought of that? It's pretty early."

He glanced at her—and a little half grin played on his lips. "I thought New York is the city that never sleeps."

She rolled her eyes. "Where did you get that? Your guidebook?"

"I wanted to learn all the local expressions and sayings before we arrived in the Big Apple," Ibrahim answered in a deadpan voice. "How am I doing?"

"Badly," she teased. "The first thing you have to do is throw out that guidebook." Her gaze shifted back to shore. The sky on the eastern horizon was now a deep, luminous blue. And she could see that in addition to a surface fog, there was something else hanging in the air . . . a faint brownish cloud that hovered over the tops of the buildings.

Gross. The corners of her mouth turned down—but she almost felt like laughing at the same time. The city really hadn't changed! It was still as polluted as ever.

"What's the matter?" Ibrahim asked.

She shook her head. "I was just looking at all the smog," she muttered. "Did the guidebook mention anything about bringing a gas mask?"

Ibrahim chuckled. "I'm sure it's nowhere near as bad as Cairo. At least they try to control it here. In the summer in Cairo you can hardly breathe."

Cairo. For some reason, hearing him talk about his former country struck a strange chord inside her. It reminded her of all the differences she had with him . . . the fact that they came from two very different cultures—two cultures, in fact, that had clashed for hundreds of years. And today she was going to introduce him to her parents.

Her mom and dad weren't exactly huge fans of Arabs.

But that was *their* problem. Sarah wouldn't let it worry her. Today was a day to rejoice. And maybe her parents had changed. The world was a very different place now.

And Sarah was a very different person.

"You know, Sarah, I was thinking about things this morning." Ibrahim's voice grew serious again. "We never found the traitor. And something else occurred to me as well. I was thinking about the code. I think it might be hidden in such a way that only *you* could find it. I know that sounds obvious, but it might be easier to find than you suspect. It might lie in the translation, in the way the scroll uses both the Western calendar and the Hebrew calendar. . . ."

But Sarah wasn't listening.

She was staring at Brooklyn. There was something *wrong* with that smog. She could see it now; the sky was getting lighter and lighter. Her heart skipped a beat. The ugly brown cloud almost looked as if it were *moving*—

"Sarah!" Ibrahim screamed. "Look!"

He spun her in the opposite direction.

Sarah's entrails turned to ice. She stopped breathing. An uncertain mass was rushing out of the blackness of Staten Island, straight toward the ship—something huge and cloudlike and buzzing, made up of millions of different specks . . . and then it was upon them. The specks were crawling over her flesh, hopping across the deck. . . .

"Bugs!" she shrieked.

Terror instantly consumed her.

Grasshoppers? She scratched at herself, reeling blindly around the deck—but there were too many of them. Her movements became more fierce, more violent. They were in her hair, on her face, on her legs.

"Sarah!" Ibrahim cried in the chaos. "Sarah, go downstairs. Get out of here!"

Her head jerked in every direction, but she couldn't seem to find him. The cloud of bugs was too thick. Kids were pouring out of doors and stairwells. Within seconds full-fledged pandemonium had erupted on the deck. The air was filled with screams and cries in half a dozen languages; everybody was kicking and shoving—

A hand grabbed her and yanked her back toward the railing.

Ibrahim! Sarah stared at him. Nausea rose in her gut. His smooth, dark skin was *covered* with bugs. There must have been twenty on his face alone.

"Listen to me," he said, spinning her and seizing her by the shoulders. "You have to get downstairs and secure the scroll. Do you understand?"

Sarah blinked. She couldn't move. She was literally frozen stiff.

"Do you understand?" he repeated.

126

Bugs fluttered between them.

All at once Aviva appeared—running in circles around the deck like a lunatic. "Save yourself, Sarah!" she shouted, pulling at her red hair. "Save yourself! You're the Chosen One! You're the only one of us who matters!"

"I . . ." Sarah dimly sensed something pulling at her—a gravitational tug. Dizziness fogged her brain; the landscape behind Ibrahim seemed to have shifted direction.

He glanced toward the front of the ship. His eyes widened.

"We're turning!" he yelled. His fingers dug into her flesh. "We're going to hit the base of the bridge! Why don't they stop?" Sarah forced herself to look.

No! Oh my—

The front of the ship slammed into a massive, graffiti-covered concrete wall. There was a high-pitched, rending screech. The deck seemed to drop from under her feet; her legs struck the railing. A stinging pain shot through her thighs. She flipped upside down and went tumbling and tumbling through empty space. Portholes rushed past her. She opened her mouth to scream, but no sound passed her lips. . . .

Splat!

Her body struck the water. Fortunately she was too numb to feel any pain. A putrid, salty stench suffused her nostrils. There was nothing but blackness—ice-cold blackness. She kicked and kicked, and after several seconds her head popped through the surface. . . .

"Sarah!"

She flailed her arms, gasping. Ibrahim must have fallen in, too. She blinked and shook her soaking hair out of her eyes. Yes—he was swimming toward her. Bugs hovered in the air below the bridge, inches over their heads.

"Stay there!" he shouted. His voice gurgled in the water as he plowed ahead.

But her clothing seemed to be weighing her down, pulling her back under. *Help me,* she thought, panicking. She hated the water; she was a terrible swimmer. She'd never admitted it to anyone. Her splashing grew more desperate, more out of control. Her arms were already tired. *Help me. Help—*

"Hold on to me," Ibrahim ordered. He was suddenly right in front of her. "Just relax. Get onto my back."

She climbed on top of him and wrapped her arms around his neck. For a horrifying instant they both sank beneath the surface. But then Ibrahim kicked his legs and they surged forward, straight toward a rocky bank. Sarah held her breath. She squeezed her eyes closed and thrust out her hand. Moments later her fingertips scraped against the rough edge of a wet stone.

Yes!

Her eyelids flew open. Ibrahim dove from underneath her. She lunged forward and seized two rocks, then tried to pull herself up out of the water. But the rocks were too slick. She couldn't get a grip on them. She kept slipping back down. . . .

"I've got you!" Ibrahim shouted. He scrambled up

beside her and planted himself firmly on a relatively even surface, then grabbed her wrists and yanked. She was shocked at his strength. He pulled her out in a matter of seconds. She collapsed on her back, panting.

"Are you all right?" Ibrahim gasped.

She nodded. "Thank you," she breathed shakily. "Thank you. Thank you—"

Ibrahim suddenly bent over.

He blinked several times, then fell to his knees.

He gazed at her . . . and his entire face slipped from his skull in a thick black liquid torrent.

"Ibrahim?" she whispered.

He gently melted into the surface of the rocks, without so much as a sound.

Ibrahim?

But there was nobody there.

He was dead. Gone.

He was here, and then he wasn't. The boy she loved was *dead*. A scream pierced the morning twilight. Sarah didn't even realize the sound was coming from her mouth. Her body was rigid, petrified—every one of her five senses focused on the horror of Ibrahim's death.

Her eyes flashed to the ship. The entire front end was crushed like a soda can; it was already listing to one side. It was going down. And the scroll was going with it. As were all her careful notes in her journal. People were already leaping into the water.

It couldn't be happening. She shook her head. It was impossible. In a manner of seconds she'd lost everything. *Everything!* Ibrahim, the scroll, the truth, the *hope* . . .

The words of the prophecy rang through her mind: *"Again the Chosen One will suffer, and again she will be saved."*

Yet she had only one thought as she stared back down at Ibrahim's remains.

Saved from what?

Sarah. Josh.

Ariel. Brian.

Harold. Julia.

George.

Don't grow too attached to them.

They won't live long.

Don't miss the next thrilling installment of
Daniel Parker's

COUNTDOWN

Official Rules
COUNTDOWN
Consumer Sweepstakes

1. No purchase necessary. Enter by mailing the completed Official Entry Form or print out the official entry form from www.SimonSays.com/countdown or write your name, telephone number, address, and the name of the sweepstakes on a 3" x 5" card and mail it to: Simon & Schuster Children's Publishing Division, Marketing Department, Countdown Sweepstakes, 1230 Avenue of the Americas, New York, New York 10020. One entry per person. Sweepstakes begins November 9, 1998. Entries must be received by December 31, 1999. Not responsible for postage due, late, lost, stolen, damaged, incomplete, not delivered, mutilated, illegible, or misdirected entries, or for typographical errors in the entry form or rules. Entries are void if they are in whole or in part illegible, incomplete, or damaged. Enter as often as you wish, but each entry must be mailed separately.

2. All entries become the property of Simon & Schuster and will not be returned.

3. Winners will be selected at random from all eligible entries received in a drawing to be held on or about January 15, 2000. Winner will be notified by mail. Odds of winning depend on the number of eligible entries received.

4. One Grand Prize: $2,000 U.S. Two Second Prizes: $500 U.S. Three Third Prizes: balloons, noise makers, and other party items (approximate retail value $50 U.S.).

5. Sweepstakes is open to legal residents of U.S. and Canada (excluding Quebec). Winner must be 20 years old or younger as of December 31, 1999. Employees and immediate family

members of employees of Simon & Schuster, its parent, subsidiaries, divisions, and related companies and their respective agencies and agents are ineligible. Prizes will be awarded to the winner's parent or legal guardian if under 18.

6. One prize per person or household. Prizes are not transferable and may not be substituted except by sponsors, in event of prize unavailability, in which case a prize of equal or greater value will be awarded. All prizes will be awarded.

7. All expenses on receipt and use of prize, including federal, state, and local taxes, are the sole responsibility of the winners. Winners may be required to execute and return an Affidavit of Eligibility and Release and all other legal documents that the sweepstakes sponsor may require within 15 days of attempted notification or an alternate winner will be selected.

8. By accepting a prize, a winner grants to Simon & Schuster the right to use his/her name and likeness for any advertising, promotional, trade, or any other purpose without further compensation or permission, except where prohibited by law.

9. If the winner is a Canadian resident, then he/she will be required to answer a time-limited arithmetical skill-testing question administered by mail.

10. Simon & Schuster shall have no liability for any injury, loss, or damage of any kind, arising out of participation in this sweepstakes or the acceptance or use of a prize.

11. The winner's first name and home state or province will be posted on www.SimonSays.com/countdown or the names of the winners may be obtained by sending a separate, stamped, self-addressed envelope to: Winner's List "Countdown Sweepstakes", Simon & Schuster Children's Marketing Department, 1230 Avenue of the Americas, New York, NY 10020.

COUNTDOWN
to the
MILLENNIUM
Sweepstakes

$2,000 for the year 2000

5...4...3...2...1 MILLENNIUM MADNESS.
The clock is ticking ... enter now to
win the prize of the millennium!

1 GRAND PRIZE:
$2,000 for the year 2000!

2 SECOND PRIZES: $500

3 THIRD PRIZES: balloons, noisemakers,
and other party items (retail value $50)